By JOHN GOODE

Last Dance with Mary Jane

TALES FROM FOSTER HIGH
Tales From Foster High
End of the Innocence
151 Days
Taking Chances
What About Everything?
By Robert Halliwell: A Way Back to Then
Save Yourself
When I Grow Up

Published by Harmony Ink Press

Jordan vs. All the Boys

FADEAWAY
Going the Distance

LORDS OF ARCADIA
Distant Rumblings
Eye of the Storm
With J.G. Morgan: The Unseen Tempest
With J.G. Morgan: Stormfront

Published by DREAMSPINNER PRESS
www.dreamspinnerpress.com

Taking Chances

John Goode

DREAMSPINNER
PRESS

Published by
DREAMSPINNER PRESS

5032 Capital Circle SW, Suite 2, PMB# 279, Tallahassee, FL 32305-7886 USA
www.dreamspinnerpress.com

Taking Chances

Cover Art

Trade Paperback ISBN: 978-1-64405-844-2
Digital ISBN: 978-1-64405-843-5
Library of Congress Control Number: 2020937736
Trade Paperback published December 2021
Second Edition
v. 2.0
Previously published by Dreamspinner Press, August 2013

Printed in the United States of America
∞
This paper meets the requirements of
ANSI/NISO Z39.48-1992 (Permanence of Paper).

AUTHOR'S NOTE

THIS BOOK takes place in the imaginary town of Foster, Texas. Tyler has been featured in my other series, *Tales from Foster High*, which is where Brad and Kyle's story can be found. This book takes place during *End of the Innocence*, Tales from Foster High: Book Two, where the events at the end of that book are dealt with in greater detail.

MATT

IF THERE is anything harder than growing up gay, it's growing up gay in Texas.

There are few places on the planet nicer than Foster, Texas, to be raised in, but as with all forms of perfection, there are some rules. There are horror films that take place in little towns like this. People find the places pleasant, with accepting and loving people who respect each other under God as long as you are exactly like them in every way that counts. But if you are different in any way, they will come at you with a fury that will remind you that we really did burn people at the stake for being witches.

It's a lot like beehive thinking, except in Foster, there was no queen, no one overriding presence that made us all do the same thing. Guys like my brothers conformed because none of them wanted to be different. They all wore the same kind of clothes, had the same short hair, and talked the same way about the things they liked.

I dressed like them, walked like them, and talked like them because, like a in beehive, the drones will attack any stranger on sight.

I remember growing up thinking I was the only person in the world who was like me. I was one of those mutants you read about in the comic books, a normal-looking person on the outside but a hideous creature just under my skin, and that forever set me apart from everyone else. My reaction was so stereotypical that I am loathe in this day and age to repeat it out loud to other gay people. I was a pariah in my own mind; the scarlet letter was invisible to others but plain as day to me—a huge pink F that followed me wherever I went, and no matter how hard I tried, I couldn't shake it.

I remember being on the edge of seventeen, that dangerous time between childhood and young adult when the concrete is still wet in your mind. That part of your life where things get stuck and form who you are for the rest of your life, wanted or not. Offhand comments, distant laughter, anything a boy's fragile ego could mistake for a slight could affect the kind of man he would one day become. There is never a time in your life when love is so sweet, pain cuts so deep, or memory is so undeniably carved in stone.

Though I am closer to forty than I am to thirty, I can still remember moments of time from when I was a teenager that are so vivid, they could have taken place yesterday. Ask me the name of the guy who talked to me at the gym last week or Sophia's boyfriend's name and I draw a blank. But ask me about the time I saw the boy down the street mow the lawn shirtless for the first time and I can still smell the cut grass and the way the sun beat down on me unmercifully. It could have been this afternoon instead of a decade ago.

And that is not always a good thing.

"So…." Sophia swirled the straw around in her glass in the same manner a cat plays with a mouse before eating it. "Home for the holidays, huh?"

I groaned as put my head down on the table. "Why won't you let this go?" I begged.

"Because, my dear friend," she teased, "sometimes I feel like I'm best friends with James Bond and not some fag hag to an uptight hick."

"I hate that word," I mumbled into the table.

"Which one?" she asked. "Hick or fag?"

"Both," I grunted.

"I know. That's why I use them," she answered airily around sips of her drink. "So spill. What's a real Texas Christmas like?"

I winced as images crowded my mind. Both my brothers and their families annually invade my parents' living room. Both of them are in some demented race to have as many offspring as they can, so I can expect a new baby to coo at and be spit up on by every other year. I end up cowering in a corner trying desperately to remember their kids' names. The stifling heat, because my mother thinks the moment I moved out of state, I lost the ability to handle a "proper North Texas winter," the painful smile I keep on my face as my sisters-in-law ask, again, "What's it like living in such an exciting place as San Francisco?" and "You must have the best time!" The entire time, I try to convince myself what they're saying isn't code for "So what's it like having a ton of gay sex in the big city?"

"Long," I said miserably as I looked up and saw the cute barista walk by and flash me what had to be a pity smile.

"And that's what she said," Sophia added, laughing at her own joke. "So when do you leave?"

"Day after tomorrow," I answered, trying to find a way to turn around and look at him without seeming like I was turning around and looking at him.

Sophia looked at me and rolled her eyes. "Just ask him out already," she said in exasperation. "Or better yet, go corner him in the bathroom!"

I tried not to blush and failed miserably. Sophia learned everything she knew about gay culture from watching *Queer as Folk* and was constantly miserable that I was nothing like the characters in the show. "He just reminds me of someone," I said as I sneaked a peek over my shoulder.

Of course, that was exactly when he walked back with a few empty cups. He smiled and stopped. "Did you need another?"

"Another what?" I blurted out, turning away and seeing the empty coffee mug in front of me. "Another coffee, obviously, because I'm in a coffee shop and what else would you be asking me about?" And then I realized I said all that out loud. My head hit the table again. "No, thank you."

Sophia cackled as the blood rushed to my head. I hated Christmas.

"He's cute," she commented while I prayed he was out of earshot.

I looked up in exasperation. "Of course he's cute. He works at a gay coffeehouse for tips." I pushed my mug away dejectedly. "The only profession that depends more on looks is a male stripper." I glanced over at him; he was smiling and taking another order behind the counter. "'Sides, he's not that cute."

"Who's not that cute?" What's-his-name asked, wiping his hands on his jeans.

"The guy behind the counter," Sophia explained to her boyfriend, whose name I still could not remember.

He looked over and then back with a lewd smile. "Oh yeah, he's hot."

I rolled my eyes and looked at Sophia. "You seriously know you're dating a gay guy, right?"

"Hey! I'm not gay!" What's-his-name said as he took a sip of his coffee. "I am an enlightened man of the times."

"You dress better than I do and are constantly pointing out cute guys," I said, tiring of this never-ending argument. "You're gayer than I am."

"That's not saying much," Sophia muttered under her breath. I pretended not to hear her.

But she was right; I was hands down the worst gay guy in the world.

The other horrible part about growing up in Foster was that I had no gay role models to speak of. There was that gay uncle on *Bewitched*, the weird guy on *Too Close for Comfort*, and Mr. Roper batting his eyelashes on *Three's Company*, but I wasn't that type of gay. I had played football since I knew how to walk and did both at about the same skill level, which was to say not very well at all. My brothers and I were all jocks in high school. Although I was the least jockish of the bunch, I still passed as more than straight to the general populace. When I moved to the West Coast, I thought I'd finally be free—able to explore my sexuality and all the joy that would come with it.

I realized I had moved from being a misfit in a culture I wasn't a part of to being a freak in the culture I was supposed to be in. I didn't believe in casual sex. I didn't like to get drunk. Bars were too loud, sweaty, and sad for my taste, and frankly, I had never met a man who could measure up to the ideal I had in my head.

"He means he's not cute compared to the boy with the red door," Sophia said with a wicked smile.

"I hate you," I said, meaning every word.

"The guy with the red what?" What's-his-name asked.

"There was this boy that lived down the street that Matt here was in *llluuuuuuuvvvvvvv* with when he was in high school." Her laughter chewed my eardrums like nails on a chalkboard. "Of course, being Matt, he never once talked to him. Matt only stalked him from afar and now judges every man he meets against that guy." What's-his-name looked over at the barista and back at me. "This guy with the red thing must have been hot."

"Okay, honey," Sophia interjected, quietly patting his arm. "Little too much sharing."

She was right. I did judge everyone against that one boy. Of course, because he was a figment of my imagination and therefore perfect, everyone else I met over the years was found wanting. That probably makes little sense, so let me try to explain it a bit better.

When I was growing up, there was a boy who lived two blocks down, and he was the reason I knew I was gay. Foster is an odd place; we are still small in terms of an actual town, but in population, there seemed to be more people than were ever seen. We were the closest thing to a real town within seventy-five miles, so Foster ended up being the hub for a few dozen towns that were too small to support a high school, and who also depended on us as a means of existence. I remember thinking that the idea of people who came to Foster for fun didn't compute in my high school mind, but it was the truth. There were enough people that we supported two different high schools, and there was no pattern on who should go to which one.

My brothers and I went to Foster High, the school that was an odd mix of yuppie kids combined with those from the wrong side of the tracks. Its buildings were aged, its textbooks and computers ragged, its uniforms were worn, and the band had trouble marching in a straight line. In every way, Foster High was and is looked down on by the students at Granada, the newer school. That made our rivalry that much fiercer. The Boy went to Granada, and because he went to Granada, he automatically became a Capulet to our Montagues.

He was a jock just like my brothers and I were, playing a variety of sports much like we did. Everyone knew him, walking down Main Street in his letterman jacket, easy smile, tattered white T-shirt that looked so soft you just wanted to touch it. He was always with friends and was always surrounded, as if the entire town wanted to touch him, be near him, draw what warmth they could from his presence. If he was comfortable with the attention, he never showed it. Instead, he always had a nervous smile on his face and unconsciously ran his fingers through that golden hair, which made the T-shirt ride up. Like a comet, that brief glimpse of skin between his shirt and jeans was worth waiting for weeks to appear.

Sophia snapped her fingers in front of my face, breaking me out of my stupor as I remembered him. "Okay, back to Earth. So, how long are you staying?"

"As little as humanly possible," I said, looking at the time and realizing I was close to being late. "Shit, I need to go."

"So does his family still live in town?" she asked as I pulled on my jacket.

"I'm not seeing him." I grabbed my messenger bag and darted for the door. "I'll call you later."

"Bye!" the cute guy behind the counter called out. I turned to see him waving at me.

I'd started to wave back when I slammed into the front door and fell onto my ass. He covered his mouth in horror as I shook my head and realized the entire place was staring at me.

"Fucking Christmas!" I cursed as scrambled to my feet and fled the scene.

For a long time, I had secretly blamed the Boy for making me different. As far as I could see, it had been his fault that something in my mind switched from girls to boys when I saw him for the first time. I might have had thoughts before, might have wondered, but it wasn't until the day I saw him mowing the lawn that I knew, I knew for sure. I wanted someone who looked just like him. And if not, as close as I could get would do.

I closed my eyes and I was there again.

It was a Saturday afternoon, one of the few he wasn't roaming free across Foster with his pack mates like they owned the town. It was obvious that he had been resigned to mowing his lawn instead of running free, and it was that day as I walked by on my way to First Street that I knew… I was never going to be the same again.

He wore a pair of blue jeans that had been old the previous year. They were frayed and faded to the point of distraction, with the band of his white boxers just hanging out, almost daring someone to comment on them. He pushed the lawnmower around as if it owed him money, he was so angry. Two white headphone wires trailed down his back as he ignored the world around him and took it out on his chores. His hair was matted from the heat, and drops of sweat trailed down his face. The world stopped spinning while I watched the sun shine down on the tanned perfection that was his shirtless form. I paused in the street, completely floored by the Adonis in front of me. And there, in the middle of the explosion in my mind, he looked up at me. Our eyes met, and if he knew why I was looking, he gave no indication. His eyes blazed under the green John Deere hat as he kept moving across the lawn… looking away slowly as if he hadn't seen me gaping at him.

I blinked and I could still see him, an afterimage burned in my mind like looking at the sun too long. That was over ten years ago, and I still saw him every time I closed my eyes.

My brothers, of course, had nothing good to say about him when I asked them if they knew who he was. He went to Granada, which meant he was obviously the enemy. They explained how he and his friends were the bad guys and that I was to tell them if he even looked at me wrong. We were teenage boys, and most of us just waited around looking for a reason to get into a fight. As the youngest, I had sworn to hate him, but seeing him there, alone for the first time, things had changed.

I had always known I was different. My brothers and their friends seemed to live for spitting, farting, and endless competitions to see who was better than the other. They would talk endlessly about girls and what they had done, what they would do, and then finally what they would settle for if they ever had the chance to be with one. Their various comparisons left me cold, though I went along with them because the alternative was sitting alone in my room longing for something I couldn't explain. I never had a name for what was inside me. No, to be honest, I never wanted to name it. I came from the old school of superstition that if you didn't give an evil a name, it couldn't quite possess you. So I never said the word out loud, never thought it to myself. I knew I was different and left it at that, but inside I craved to be like my brothers and their friends so bad, I just ignored it and hoped one day it would pass. But seeing him there, shirtless, sweat pouring down every muscle he had, the feeling inside me suddenly received a name, and it wasn't one I liked.

BY THE time I walked into work, all I could think of was the Boy. I wondered if his family still lived in Foster. The whole morning, if I had more than thirty seconds to myself, my attention would drift back to that day when I knew I was sexually attracted to him, and not in a small way. After that, I thought I was so obvious that everyone in town was just being nice to me while laughing behind my back the whole time. They had to have noticed the way I stared too long or looked away too fast. The way I got too loud when the conversation turned to sex or the way I seemed to have no interest in girls at all. Everything I did and said was under a veil of self-scrutiny, looking for any hint that I was less of a man than the rest of them. After a while, I began talking about girls, loudly and awkwardly. I tried drinking beer in the back of whichever pickup I was riding in on our way to the lake, and I even asked a girl to the Winter Formal.

None of it made me any straighter.

My phone rang in my office, dispelling my memories for the moment.

"Matt Wallace," I answered, trying to banish the Ghost of Adolescence Past from my brain.

"Matty?" my mother's voice asked through the phone. "Matty, is that you?"

"Hi, Mom," I answered, silently groaning because I knew what call this was.

"Are you busy? I know it's the afternoon."

My mother comes from the generation that believes the afternoon is for work and work only. It means you were either busy working or busy trying to avoid work. She didn't understand how I could sit in an office every day wearing a suit and dealing with computers and still have more than enough spare time to talk on the phone and not get in trouble.

"I'm fine, Mom. What's up?" I assured her, knowing without it she would never get to the reason she called.

"Where are you?" she asked.

"I'm at work, Mom. You called me," I said, trying to keep the shortness out of my voice.

"Well, I don't know how this thing works!" she complained, meaning she was on the cell phone I had bought her last year. "I'm afraid I'm going to break it sometimes."

"I'm at work and it's fine, Mom," I said, trying to focus her before she went off on a tangent about technology today being purposely overcomplicated.

"Well, I just got off the phone with Teresa"—that was my oldest brother's wife—"and she was checking in for Christmas, and I realized I hadn't heard from you yet. You are coming, right?" She asked in the same way a mob boss would ask if I understood that we were family and family had certain obligations.

"Yes, Mother," I said, trying not to sigh. "I emailed you my itinerary."

"Well, that thing doesn't work the way it's supposed to!" she exclaimed, which was her way of saying she had received my message but had been unable to decipher it.

I bit my cheek to keep from explaining it was a brand-new computer, which I knew because I had bought it for them for my father's birthday. I knew the words would fall on deaf ears. She no more understood that the computer was top-of-the-line than she understood what I did as a tech editor for a blog. There were simply too many words in that sentence that just made no sense to her. It was easier to blame the machine and use it as an excuse to call me and ask what she was after instead.

"I fly in Thursday," I said, checking my own email to make sure I had the times right. "I arrive in Dallas around 4:00 p.m. your time."

"Do you need us to pick you up from the airport?"

"I'm renting a car when I land, Mom." I was getting snippy, because she was drawing the call out longer than usual.

"Okay! Don't snap my head off." We were quiet for several seconds. She waited for me to give her an opening to ask me "the question," and I waited for her to realize I wasn't going to. Finally, she gave in. "So are you coming alone?"

And there it was.

I could never figure out if she was asking because she was concerned I was alone or that she was worried I would bring a guy with me one year. Either way, the question annoyed me, and I was unable to keep it out of my tone. "You know I am, Mom."

"Well, fine," she said, obviously exasperated. "I was just asking."

She was prying and she knew it.

"And I answered." I tried to end the call before it became an actual thing.

"You know, my friend Frances has a son who is—" She paused, still unable to say it out loud. "—too. Maybe you know him?"

I was done. "Yes, I do know him. I saw him at the last Gay Men with Pushy Mothers meeting. He's a nice guy. We're getting married next month."

Now I could almost hear the irritation radiating from her. "Well, excuse me for trying to understand your life! I'll go now and stop bugging you."

"Mom, you're not…," I began to recant.

"See you Thursday," she said as if I'd never spoken and hung up.

I slammed the phone down and tried not to scream, "*Fucking Christmas!*"

From the way people stared at me, I'm pretty sure I failed.

The rest of the day sucked. I tried unsuccessfully to focus on the work at hand and not on a boy I had seen a decade ago and never forgotten. It wasn't until I got home and called Sophia to tell her how my day had gone that I had time to actually take a breath.

"Going postal at your job?" Sophia quipped. "They'll all say you seemed like such a nice boy."

I was lying on my comically undersized couch with my calves resting on the edge. I had bought it in a fit of "trying to be metropolitan" and paid the price for it. It cost too much money, was out of style the second I got it home, and it barely fit a man half my size. I was what Sophia called corn-fed, which sounded dangerously close to fat. Sophia assured me that it meant "hot."

I didn't feel hot.

"And you'd show up at my funeral looking like what's-her-name from *Fight Club*: black makeup, shades, chain-smoking up a storm. And they'd wonder where I ever met such an ugly drag queen."

"Fuck off!" she shrieked in my ear. "And it's Helena Bonham Carter, you jackass. She is in, like, every other movie we watch."

"Every movie you pick, you mean."

She paused, mock outrage in her voice. "I'm not the one who wants to see every single sci-fi or cartoon piece of shit that comes out! It's like being friends with a twelve-year-old. At least I try to interject some culture into your hick ass."

It was true. I had no culture.

I'd remained largely unchanged since I moved from Foster, the only difference being that I now knew where gay men were but was still single. The gay scene was too loud for me, it was boisterous and rowdy, and every weekend seemed to be an excuse for someone or other to throw another idiotic party. None of it made any sense to me. What was a White Party and how was it different from a Red Party? I was pretty sure the difference had to do with sex, but there was no way I was going to ask anyone to find out for sure.

"So you were nasty to your mom." Sophia prompted me out of my thoughts.

"I wasn't nasty," I lied, knowing I had indeed been nasty. "It was the yearly 'Do I have to worry about my son dying single?' phone call. Believe me, that gets old."

"She cares."

I sighed deeply. "She cares insomuch that she can't find a way to control my life like she does with my brothers. It would be better if she would scold me for making Jesus cry because I'm having congress with the beast and move on, but she isn't even that religious."

"You having congress with anyone, much less a beast, would be a freaking miracle."

"Shut up," I snapped.

"I mean it! Walking on water seems pale in comparison to the Great White Matt getting his groove on."

She was baiting me, but I didn't have the energy to rise to it. "What are you and What's-his-name doing tonight?" I asked in an attempt to change the subject.

"You know his name is—" Something I forgot the second she said it. Arthur? Lance? Clay? Harold? I just couldn't keep it in my head. "I don't know why you refuse to remember it." Hearing annoyance in her voice was petty revenge, but it was all the justice coming my way for the night.

"Because in another four months you'll find him in bed getting fucked by some guy from the gym, and you'll say you had no clue he was secretly gay and I'll have to hear it."

She was quiet for so long I thought she might have hung up. Finally, in a soft voice she said, "That is a horrible thing to say, Matt."

And instantly I felt like shit.

"Why do you automatically assume he's a bottom? That is just cruel."

Her laughter was like a witch's curse.

"Good night," I said, knowing I had been outplayed.

"Have fun in the country!" she said before I hung up.

As I drifted off to sleep, my mind, of course, went to the past.

FOR THE rest of that summer, I discovered and invented reasons to walk past his house every day—twice a day, if I could manage it. In reality, everything that counted in town lay one hundred and eighty degrees from the direction I headed, but I began taking the long way, which was pretty much two blocks up, pass his house, and then turn around back toward town, just for a chance I could see him. A right turn past his house, another right turn on Elm Street, and a straight line back into town, all of this just for a chance to see him.

Most of the time, I made the trip fruitlessly. I might as well have been looking for some kind of mythical creature. I only caught glimpses of him, never a full-on sighting like the one I'd had the first Saturday. I was pretty sure if anyone caught me, I'd be dead. The only logical reason to pass by his house was that I was a secret fag and wanted to commit unnatural acts on his body. "Secret fag" were the exact words that pounded through my head every time I passed by his house. They would be the exact words my mother would use when she explained to my father what I had been doing when I got picked up by the police. My father, knowing he had already raised two strapping young straight men, would realize he should have stopped at a duo and lock me in the basement.

All they'd have needed to do was tell anyone who asked that they never had a third son; it had been a neighborhood friend of my brothers, and people had just assumed he was related. Or I had been farmed out to do menial tasks by a cruel uncle and had finally returned home to take over plowing the fields on the home farm, literally. I would have spent the rest of my life in the cellar, wondering what the real world was like.

None of that stopped me from passing his home as many times as I could.

The house wasn't as large as ours, but it had a big backyard, surrounded by what looked like a homemade wooden fence that had seen better times. It was like a house that had given up on trying to be anything more than just a place to live. The cracks through the fence didn't show much of the backyard. It wasn't easy to see back there, but from what I could tell, they didn't use the backyard for anything more than storage. The trees were overgrown, casting the entire area in perpetual shadow, discarded toys, a few bikes. It wasn't dirty per se; it just wasn't perfect like my dad kept ours. The only thing I could see clearly was the back door.

It was red.

More accurately, the door must have been red at one point. By the time I saw it that summer, time and use had worn the color almost away, and it was a door that had been red. Nothing about the door, the house, or the yard was trashy. Instead, everything looked worn, as if better days had come and gone. After more than a week of passing by his house, hoping to see him mowing the lawn or perhaps doing jumping jacks in just a pair of gym shorts, or whatever my hormone-laden mind could conjure up, I was losing hope. After a while I began to wonder if I had imagined him. That whatever sickness had taken up residence in my loins had used its powers to manifest erotic illusions of a half-naked boy doing chores in hopes of driving me insane.

If that was the plan, it was working.

On afternoons we didn't have practice, I would ditch my brothers and take my roundabout shortcut past his place, my fingers crossed he'd be there. If I couldn't see him out front, I would move around to the side and check through the holes in the fence. Like a junkie scrambling for another hit, I would peer into the darkness of the backyard in hopes of just one more glimpse, one more image.

And one day, he was there.

If I hadn't been so surprised and frozen on the spot, I would have given myself away. He was leaning up against the door, reading a book and looking so relaxed, he reminded me of stumbling across a doe grazing in a private glade that, instead of running, just looked up at you in curiosity. He had taken his shoes off, and for some reason, seeing him barefoot was akin in my mind to catching him nude. He was so undeniably beautiful that my standards of what a handsome male looked like were forever changed.

THAT IMAGE was the first thing that came to mind when I woke up the next morning and got ready to leave for Foster.

I checked in to my flight early, not wanting to be caught in a random airport pat down that would make me miss my flight. I could be brought up on terrorist charges, and I know my mom would find a way to say I did it on purpose just to get out of coming home for Christmas. One of the few perks of reviewing high-tech gadgets for a living was the free stuff you got from people wanting to see their product on our site. The tablet I was using was one of those perks. I sat at my gate and checked my email as I waited.

A short email from Sophia wished me a good flight and said she was crossing her fingers for me to find a package of sex under the tree. She knew I was unhappy, had been unhappy, and was most likely going to continue being unhappy if nothing changed.

WHEN I moved away from Foster, I'd been so sure that getting out was going to change everything. The truth was that there was no one to date in Nowhere, Texas. The only gay guy in town was the old man who ran the florist shop, and he acted more like a perv than an actual person. There was always talk by people of random hookups in the park, and once I even heard about a rest stop about ten miles out of town you could find sex at. Of course no one had seen this for themselves; like alligators in the sewers and people dying by saying Bloody Mary in front of a mirror, they were all just urban legends for Foster, and I needed more than that.

I had dated girls in high school for the same reason I wore white T-shirts and rolled up the cuffs of my jeans: because it was what my brothers did. I dated an average-looking girl who knew dating one of the Wallace brothers was a step up in our little social circle. Since my brothers actually liked girls, they had already picked out the best-looking ones they could score. I was like an old lady picking out a new car; I didn't much care what it looked like as long as it was reliable.

And the girl had been reliable.

She also had thought I was the sweetest guy on earth, since I never tried to paw her and was neater than any three boys she knew. I remember her kissing me at the dance and me wondering how it would feel to kiss the boy behind the red door. I had caught him a few more times after school, alone, reading, as silently contemplative as a Greek god. I'd die to know what it was he read, why he was alone, and if I would ever know his name.

I'm not sure if this girl knew I liked guys, but she figured out quickly enough I didn't like her. But she didn't much care, and it became a *de facto* arrangement. She wore my class ring and said she was dating a Wallace boy. I had her ring on a chain so I could say I was dating a girl. We both got something out of it, but we both lost a lot more as it went on.

"Sir," a voice said as I was nudged.

I opened my eyes and realized I had slept from takeoff to landing. It was just me and the nice flight attendant who, no doubt, wanted to get the drooling idiot off her plane so she could leave. She smiled and said, "We've landed, sir."

"Thank you," I mumbled. I pushed myself to my feet and was snapped back into my seat; the seat belt was still doing its job. I almost knocked the breath out of myself as I struggled to free myself from the belt and the embarrassment. The attendant reached down and opened it with one flick of her wrist. I grabbed my bag and slunk out of the plane with what little dignity I still possessed.

After grabbing my luggage, I exited the terminal and was caught unprepared by how cold it was. Everyone likes to think Texas is a hot place, but no one who lives through a Texas winter thinks that for long. I half ran to catch the bus to the rental car lot and tried to breathe life into my hands as we drove. When I got into the car, I blasted the heater as far as it could go and just waited for something that resembled warmth. By the time I'd finished shivering, the vents began to sputter out something that wasn't cold air in my face. Still shivering because I'd grabbed the icy steering wheel, I put the car into gear and left the parking lot.

Driving to Foster was like driving back in time, except I didn't have to go eighty-eight miles an hour or have that crazy guy from *Taxi* yelling at me all the time.

There were slight differences here and there, but you could have taken a picture of Foster ten years ago and transposed this image over it and not come up with many changes at all. The Vine had a new marquee, which looked a lot like the old one with more lights. I saw that they had put a stoplight in where Railroad Avenue intersected First Street, but besides that, the same. I suddenly felt like a teenager again, the town closing in on me as my own private shame began to shrink away from the light. This was why I hated coming back. Not because my mother bugged me or because I didn't want to see my family. Foster, the town itself, made me feel so damn bad about being gay, it was all I could do to stop myself from screaming out loud for people to get the fuck out of my face.

Sophia would have brought up that no one was even close to being in my face. And she would have been right. That was what made it worse. I knew that no one here knew a thing about me or cared about the person I actually was. But there was such a paranoia that they might that from the moment I touched down, I began counting the seconds until I left again. I had just gotten here and I already wanted to leave. I think that was a new record for me.

I passed Foster High, and I could see the football field from the road. I had spent most of my high school life on that field, training, running, playing, wishing I wasn't on it. My junior year, the coaches from Foster and Granada decided that we should play a preseason game, which was really just a lame excuse for a grudge match. It was the only time we met on the field, since we both played in different leagues to prevent the rivalry from becoming even worse than it already was. I remember being torn between apprehension because their team seemed so much better than ours, and anticipation because I'd be seeing *him* somewhere else than behind his house. He was a running back, and I remember the moment I saw him in those football pants and pads, I nearly popped a bone right there on the line. Even though he never directly looked at me, I could tell it was him. I could see his eyes burning in his helmet as he surveyed us lining up against him. He didn't look scared, he didn't look nervous; if anything, he looked like he had been expecting more of us.

We lost that game 42-17, and my brother said I spent more time watching Granada make plays than actually stopping them. That was true in more ways than he could ever know. The Boy moved like a panther out there. He was easily the fastest guy on either team and he knew it. Even though he was as intense as any three players I had ever seen, I could see such joy in his face when he sat on the sidelines and watched his defense play. Even though we lost, I knew I had fallen in love a little bit more with him.

I remember seeing his last name on the back of his jersey, Parker, which instantly became my favorite last name, and I am now well-practiced writing Matt Parker in my notebook when bored. I heard he had gotten a scholarship, and the next year I read in the paper he had been accepted to Florida to play for them. One day he was there and the next he was simply gone, and my life had never been the same since then.

When I moved to the Bay Area, I had met a lot of guys looking to date. I wasn't shy to use an app to find other guys who seemed to be like-minded, and more than a few were more than willing to meet a former Texas football player who was fresh off the bus, as they say. They were all great guys. Well, not great, but at the very least decent guys.

Each one, in his own personal way, tried to get me to adjust to gay life. And each one, in his own little fucked-up way, made me hate it even more. They weren't masculine enough or weren't monogamous enough or wanted to party too much or just weren't him. At first, I simply thought there were just no decent guys out there. And then Sophia said the smartest thing that ever fell out of her mouth.

"With so many guys hooking up around here and you always single, maybe the problem isn't them, but you."

I really hated it when she was right.

I slowed as I passed his house, my car taking me by there before my brain even knew where I was going. The house looked the same but smaller, almost as if time itself had worn it down evenly and left a smaller yet identical house in the same place. The backyard still looked overgrown, but the fence was new. I wondered who lived there now, and if they would ever know how much a red door can affect someone's life.

There were two cars already parked in front of my parents' house, which meant again, I was the last to arrive. Walking into the house last during holidays was like walking late into class. You knew you were disturbing something you were supposed to be a part of, and everyone was looking at you, wondering why the hell you were so late.

Have I mentioned I hated Christmas?

I grabbed my bags and made my way up the walk. By the time I got to the door, my oldest brother had swung it open and was glaring at me. I paused, understanding I was not going to pass until he had his say, and from the way he swayed slightly and the smell about him, he was going to have about half a six-pack worth of stuff to say.

"You're a real asshole, you know that?" he declared, closing the door behind him.

In my defense, I did know that.

"You upset Mom when all she's doing is checking up on you. You're late again, showing up with your matching luggage and your fancy clothes. Don't think I don't know about you, what you really think."

"John?" I interrupted him. "There is a point to this, right?"

"You think you're better than us," he spit out as if I'd never spoken. "You always thought you were better than us—don't think we didn't notice. Little Mr. I'm Too Good For All This thinking he's too good for all this."

I might have misjudged by about five or six beers.

"And let me guess, you show up with your fancy presents and high-fangled gadgets, making the rest of our gifts look like crap!" He jabbed me in the chest with a finger. John had let himself go like my older brother. What was once muscle and lean was now larger and slightly flabby. Both were handsome in their own way, but it was obvious their best days were behind them, and that was sad to me.

"I bought you guys an iPad," I said, hoping to derail this fight before it got some steam under it.

"You did?" he exclaimed as his face lit up. "You did that for me?" And he hugged me.

I didn't have the heart to say I did that for both of them, but it stopped a fight, so I didn't argue.

"Come on already!" He gestured toward the door as if I were the one who had stopped him. "They're all waiting for ya!"

He took my bags and busted in, yelling, "Guess who finally decided to show up?"

There was a cheer, but it sounded fake to me as I closed the door behind me. I tried to ignore the feeling it was a cell door.

I had been miserable being gay in Foster and moved out as soon as I could. I went to school in Berkeley, which was the farthest school in distance and philosophy from Texas that I could find. I ended up meeting a group of guys who were making a website that needed content, and eight years later I was the tech editor for what was considered *the* word on consumer electronics. It was a good job and it was a good life, but it wasn't a happy one, and I couldn't figure out why. It drove me crazy to have a hole in the center of my life that I couldn't fill with anything I put in there.

Wow, did that sound bad.

I tried money, but all it did was make my place look crowded. I tried sex, but all it made me was feel guilty. I tried exercise, but all that did was make the sex easier to get. Finally I settled on being quietly miserable, waiting for the next part of my life to begin. But at almost forty, I was wondering how much more was left. My brothers were only a few years older, and they had lives and families and mortgages, and they seemed perfectly fine. I wanted to be perfectly fine, but it wasn't in the cards. So I sat in my parents' living room and prepared to be miserable until the weekend ended, when I could go home and be miserable there.

About an hour into catching up, William, my middle brother, came over and sat next to me. "So did you really get John an iPad?" he asked in a low voice, as if we were in a spy novel.

I nodded as I forced myself to take another drink of my father's toxic eggnog. "I got you one too," I said, knowing what he was fishing for.

"*Yes!*" he said, pumping his arm. "Hey, look, I know you know this stuff. I got the kids this video game thing, but I don't know how it works. Does it need batteries?"

I counted to an unimaginably high number in my head as I tried not to snap at him. "You are going to have to be a little more specific than a 'video game thing' for me to answer, Will."

He drew back as if I had swung at him. "What's wrong with you?"

I finished the drink and sighed. "Jetlag. Where is it?"

"It's in the trunk of my car. I just need to know if it needs anything else, 'cause you know if they can't hook it up on Christmas, they are going to burn the house down…."

I was already standing up. "I'll check it out. Pop the trunk on your car."

He jumped up and slapped my back hard enough to knock a molar out if I had one loose. "You're the best, bro."

My mom gave me a glance as one of the wives told her about one of the grandkids' experience at school. Even though it was half a second, she said plenty. "I'll be right back," I said, assuring her I wasn't making a run for it and skipping town.

I wasn't surprised to find one of the cheapest game systems on the market sitting in the trunk. My brother was a good man, but with four kids, there would need to be three of him to cover the costs of those monsters. This was a perfectly acceptable system five years ago, and no doubt, since he knew nothing about it, he thought he was getting a deal on it. I knew for a fact, the company had already released the next generation of this console, which meant my brother had spent his hard-earned money on an electronic Edsel.

I hauled it and the few games they had bought out of the trunk and took it all over to my car. Just on the outskirts of town there was an outlet mall with a Best Buy, which meant I could still save Christmas for my nephews.

I found it funny that all the modern-day stores had been built outside of town. It always felt as if Foster itself was a historical monument to an age gone by and no one, not even Walmart, could blemish it with a sign. The slow bustle of the town was replaced by hordes of angry cars as they all tried to edge into the store parking lot, intent on last-minute Christmas shopping. This was where all the small-town charm and atmosphere evaporated and the real face of its people was revealed. I heard a symphony of blaring horns and outraged shouts, and for a second, it reminded me of California.

I parked on the edge of the lot and grabbed the system and its bags. I saw a Toys for Tots display in the front window; a young, fresh-faced Marine stood there making me feel old and perverted in one fell swoop as I approached him. He saw what I had in my hand and looked away—no way anyone was going to donate a video game system for needy kids. I was very satisfied with his look of shock when I put it gently in the box.

"Thank you, sir!" he said with a reverence I thought absurd, considering what he did for a living.

"Merry Christmas," I said, trying to remember if I was ever that young.

Dating in San Francisco as a young man fresh from living his entire life in Foster had been like being a star attraction in a restaurant. You were the main focus of a bunch of hungry people. I wish I could say I stood by my guns and looked for love, but going nineteen years with only my good right hand to pleasure myself had made me a desperate man.

I dove into sex like some people dove into a hobby.

I tried it all, top, bottom, sideways. I had one guy talk me into a three-way, which seemed like two people too many at times. Some guy gave me poppers, which made me think I was going to pass out and have my kidney harvested. I was a fresh face with just the right lack of common sense to believe people and what they said. But no matter who I met or what we did, it was never enough. I always found fault with them in some way, secretly wondering what it would have been like with *him*. My boy behind the red door. Even after I swore off the whole dating scene, he was the center of my sex life. I had masturbated imagining him in every way possible. I felt sometimes like he was a porn star rather than a real person.

I wandered the store looking for the gifts my brothers wished they could have bought their kids, all the while avoiding the crowd the best I could. This was the other problem I had with Christmas: the sheer consumer rage it seemed to bring out in people in places like this. Like finding the right gift here would somehow make up for 364 days of them being complete assholes to everyone they knew. So when they saw that *one* thing that might save their eternal soul, they went at it with a religious zeal that left me cold.

I put the new video game system in my cart and began to wander toward the games in a leisurely pace. I was in no hurry to return to the house, and there were few places I felt more sure of myself than in an electronics store.

By the time I'd met Sophia, I had built an image in my head of a person who could in no real way exist. I had taken this image of a random boy who lived down the street and elevated him to an almost mythical status in my mind, and there was no way anyone in the world could compete with it. Sophia and What's-his-name had set me up with more than a few of their friends, and each date had ended worse than the last. I'm not sure what they found attractive in me, but I had a list of things that repulsed me about them. I had gone from a fresh-faced newbie to a stuck-up bitch in less than a year, and no one wanted to charge at that particular windmill to see if they'd somehow pass the magical checklist I carried in my head. It was Sophia getting me completely trashed one night that dragged the truth out of me. One long, slobbering, mournful night where I howled at the injustice of a world that would show me such perfection and then dare to snatch it away from me in one deft movement.

I think it was then she figured out how fucked-up I was, and it secretly thrilled her. Straight girls don't befriend gay guys because they want another "girl" to hang with or because they like being dragged to a bar full of attractive guys who won't look twice at them. They are friends with us for the drama. We are the very epitome of a CW show. We have angst, we're attractive, in shape, and dress nicely, and there is *always* a fight just on the horizon. The only thing we lack is a montage opening sequence set to upbeat '80s synth music as we all turn and smile into the camera. I know she meant well, but there were times I think Sophia liked me miserable, because a Matt in a stable and healthy relationship would not be able to distract her from What's-his-name and his ever-deflating heterosexuality.

"Matt?" a voice called out.

I turned toward the voice, wondering if it was one of the half dozen acquaintances I still knew in town. Guys who had been on the team with my brothers and me and considered me like the mascot of the team. Even though we were all pushing forty soon, I knew I'd always be referred to as Little Matty and get an affectionate hand messing up my hair. I readied my politest smile, the one I kept packed away for holidays in Foster. Or worse, it was one of my mother's friends, who I had to be triple-nice to, because if there was anything worse than me taking a strange man and bedding him on First Street while the people at Nancy's Diner watched, it would be giving off an attitude to one of her friends I met in a store. The story would be all over town in no time about Jocelyn's youngest and how he grew up such a snob and I saw him at the Best Buy and he was just so ugly to me. That's the problem with those Wallace boys. Walking around too good for this place; they get that from their mother. Et cetera, et cetera, et cetera.

By the way, if I did have sex in front of Nancy's, the worst I would hear about it would be a complaint from Gayle that she couldn't see all the good parts, and a performance note from Old Man Scarsdale, who'd fucked whores overseas in WWII and could tell you stories that would make your dick fall off.

I turned and realized I was in the middle of having a stroke.

I knew it was a stroke because I couldn't talk and I was seeing him walking toward me. It was impossible in every way possible, of course, for a few salient reasons.

Linear time does not allow for people to not to be affected by its passage, and since it had been ten years since he had looked like that, impossible.

In my entire life, I have never been so lucky as to have an event that was as astronomical as seeing him again so randomly occur. And turning around and seeing him would be akin to winning three lotteries back to back, so it was impossible.

I looked like shit and was in no way ready to see him. Not impossible, but it was a pretty strong point for me.

And then the bubble of time seemed to pop, and I saw him take two steps forward and age subtly right in front of my eyes. I could see his eyes and smile stay static as his face seemed to fill out, making him even more handsome. A fact that, if you had asked me ten seconds ago, I would have sworn was also impossible.

I stood with my mouth half-open, not sure what to say or do. Part of me wanted to run, part of me wanted to kiss him, another part of me wanted to do something else but then heard the suggestion of kissing him and changed its vote to that. He still walked with the same confidence that bordered on arrogance but was undeniably sexy. It was a slight bowlegged movement that was as distracting as it was enticing. I willed my eyes not to drift downward as he came up and thrust his hand out at me.

"Matt, Matt Wallace, right?" he asked, unsure since I in no way had acknowledged his words. I just stood there and mutely nodded, wondering where all the blood that was draining from my face might be going. "It's me," he said, as if someone could have forgotten him even for a second. "Tyler? Tyler Parker?"

And he stopped being the boy behind the red door and became Tyler.

TYLER

IF THERE is anything worse than being gay in a small town, it's being popular in that small town and no one knowing you're gay.

Growing up, I had always been in love with the concept of superheroes. Batman, Superman, as a kid I ate that shit up. My mom has a couple dozen pictures of me running around in the backyard with a towel around my neck, arms out, desperately willing myself to take flight. As I got older, I would always grab a comic from the rack when we went to get a Coke after Little League practice, but as I got closer to junior high and the hormones started to kick in, they lost their appeal really fast.

I wasn't stupid. While my friends were tripping over themselves when a girl walked by, I was doing my level best not to stare at them as we changed out. I willed myself to like girls, any girl. I had liked girls growing up, I mean, like them as elementary kids liked each other. Now it was different. The feelings I had for guys weren't about holding hands and sharing secrets. As I barreled into high school, I realized I liked guys in a carnal way, and that was the equivalent of finding out you were a serial killer in a place like Foster.

So I did what any kid in a place like this does. I created another version of myself. A straight version of myself. A version of myself that fit what my outside looked like. To anyone else I was simply Tyler Parker, all-American jock, football player, totally straight guy who liked girls just like everyone else.

While inside I was simply miserable.

So I spent my entire high school life being that Tyler Parker, star running back from Granada High, while the other me sat in the back of my mind, slowing dying a day at a time.

Yeah, superheroes and secret identities, I wasn't a fan anymore.

The only person who knew I liked guys in high school was my best friend, Linda Stilleno. She had tried to go out with me my sophomore year and ended up figuring out my secret. At first I was terrified, because with one word she could end my high school life, but I soon realized having at least one person to talk to made all the difference in the world.

"You're quiet," Linda observed when I had said nothing for several minutes.

The Rodeo Club was a local bar a block away from the sporting goods store my dad had owned and run for forty years. When he and Mom decided to retire to Florida, Dad deeded the store to me. Linda had dropped by the store at closing and asked if I wanted to get a beer with her. Since my options consisted of going home, changing my clothes and heading to the YMCA to work out, going home to my childhood house and staring blankly at TV until I went to sleep, or just going home to watch some porn while I got off before I went to sleep, I decided to go with Linda.

This was what my life had boiled down to lately.

"My mom called me," I told her and examined the label on my beer intently, not wanting to make eye contact.

"They want you to fly to Florida for Christmas?" She gestured for another round for us.

I shook my head. "They did, but I told them how much money we make over the holidays and the shop couldn't afford it."

"What did they say?"

"My mom said come anyways, but there's no way we can make that money up."

We sat there in silence, me milking my beer and her staring at me expectantly.

"Is there something wrong with your parents?"

"No."

"The store in trouble?"

"No."

She grabbed the beer out of my hand to make me look at her. "I swear to God, Tyler, if you don't tell me why you are pouting, I am going to shove this bottle so far up—"

"Okay!" I said, cutting her off before she could finish the sentence. "She also called me to tell me someone is gay."

That made her pause.

"Someone from Foster," I added, hoping she would get it.

"Someone we knew?" she prompted patiently. She and I had pretty much hung out with the same crowd growing up. Since we didn't as adults, she knew the person had to have been someone from the past. I nodded. "Who?"

The thought that maybe I shouldn't just blurt out someone's sexuality because my friend asked passed my mind way too late to do any good. Now that I'd started, I couldn't *not* talk about it, so I just shrugged and said, "Matt Wallace."

She stared at me for a few seconds before saying, "Um, yeah, everyone knows that."

Now it was my turn to stare. "Everyone?" I asked, disbelieving.

She laughed and passed my half-empty beer back to me. "He went to Berkeley for college and ended up moving to San Francisco. If he isn't gay, then he went an awful long way to be straight."

The bartender put down two bottles and took her empty away. I waited until he was out of earshot before I spoke. "You know not everyone in San Francisco is gay, right?"

She took a long swig of her beer. "The ones who aren't just can't afford to move. Trust me, he's gay." Suddenly, all the light bulbs in her brain went on at the same time. Sitting up straighter, Linda seemed to think about it for a few seconds before asking, "Wait, how does your mother know?"

Now she was getting it.

"My mom talks to his mom." I sounded like a condemned man. All I needed was a slow, deep drumbeat under my words.

"Oh no," she said, finally realizing what I was so quiet about.

I'd spent most of high school going out with girls, trying to hide my true nature. Because I was on the football team and I looked like I did, it wasn't that hard to find someone to go out with. I never stayed with one girl because there wasn't any way I could keep up the charade for any length of time. My game of musical girlfriends gave me a reputation as a player in town, not a bad player, because I never hit on them, but a player.

Which, of course, my mom defined as "Tyler just hasn't found the right girl yet."

My mother took it upon herself to be my own little matchmaker, a job she somehow changed into a crusade. Since I was too afraid to come out, there wasn't much I could say, so I just endured her efforts. And like any good mother, she took my silence as a sign of acceptance.

Then I got a football scholarship to Florida.

Once I had moved out of state, the most my mom could do was ask me endless questions about my love life. The questioning was about as uncomfortable as you might imagine. I went out with a couple of girls my freshman year. I had less of a problem selling my "player" vibe in Florida. People expected that guys on the team were going to sleep around. I really thought I was going to survive college without having to make a serious commitment to a girl. Then I caught a forty-three-yard pass late in the fourth quarter against Virginia. I got hit so hard that I literally lost consciousness for a moment.

When I woke up, I was looking up at the sky and my left leg was twisted in a way the human leg was not designed for.

I lost my scholarship and had to relearn how to walk. That sounds painful, but it was nothing compared to seeing my dad's face when he found out I was never going to play football again. It was a horrible moment and, in my opinion, one of the lowest moments of my life. Everything in my life had been wound up in being "The football guy." As long as I had to play football, I had no reason to come out, and as long as I had no reason to come out, I could just not tell anyone who I really was and live like that until I died. But as I was carried off the field, I knew the jig was up. I had nowhere else to hide.

I returned to Foster, learned how to walk without a limp, and tried to move forward.

Which was, of course, a cue for my mom to open her matchmaking service again.

My parents had planned for years to retire and move to Florida, leaving the store to me. So my mom knew the time she had left to get me married was quickly coming to an end. I kept trying to make excuses, and she thought I was retreating from people because I was depressed about my accident, but it was so much more than that. She kept pushing, I kept dodging, and then one night I just snapped.

Which was how my parents found out I was gay.

My dad went a little nuts, but not in a bad way. He just could not handle that his only son, his pride and joy, liked guys. I suppose he went through the normal stages every dad must when they find out their son is gay. Denial: *There is no way you can be gay; you dated girls.* Anger: *How can you do that to your mother? You know how much she wanted grandchildren.* More denial: *Maybe it's just a phase. Have you thought of that?* Bargaining: *Maybe you just haven't found the right girl. There are lots more girls out there.* A little more denial: *But you seemed so happy with your girlfriends.* Depression: *Was it something I did wrong? Something I could have done better?* The last bit of denial: *But I saw you kiss girls.*

It was my mother, though, who finally brought some kind of acceptance.

She had no male ego to overcome, no illusions that I was some über athlete. In her eyes, I was her baby and that was all that counted. She took Dad out one afternoon, and they had a talk. To this day, I have no idea what she said to him, but when they returned to the house, Dad was changed. He stopped complaining about it, and we went back to relating to each other through sports.

My mother didn't even pause in her quest to find me a mate. She just moved to another gender. Every week there was another article about gay rights lying on the table for me to read. She began by zeroing in on the physical therapists who worked with me to rehabilitate my leg. While we did slow-motion quad extensions, she launched a series of completely unsubtle and exhaustive questions about their sexual orientation. After a month, the in-home agency began sending only girls to our house. I'm pretty sure some of the guys complained about sexual harassment.

Undeterred, my mom continued her search.

Which brought me back to my current problem.

"Does she know Matt Wallace lives out of state?" Linda asked, snapping me out of my stupor.

"She has to," I answered miserably. "Which means she is either trying to get me to move or set me up with a hookup."

I found no humor in that statement at all, but Linda seemed to find an endless vein of humor as she began to laugh louder than the music.

"Knock it off," I said, trying to quiet her as I nervously looked around the small bar. "You're going to attract attention."

She wiped tears from her eyes as she swallowed her next round of mirth. "You *do* know it's bad when your mom's trying to get you laid for Christmas. A sure sign you are wound up too tight."

"I am not wound up too tight," I protested, but we both knew I was lying through my teeth.

I had tried being gay in Foster. I had met gay friends; I had tried to be normal. I had tried… whatever. In the end I did what I always did: I fucked things up and just made things worse.

When my parents moved away and left me the store, I hid behind the responsibility so I could give up on dating altogether. Not that I had a lot of choice; there was no way I could go back to the Bear's Den, and there was just no other way to meet gay people around here. I leaned on the internet, drove to Dallas every few weekends to meet up and have some crazy hookup sex, and then never call the guy again. It sounds cruel, but trust me, I was doing them a favor. I had given up on the concept of dating altogether. I was going to die single, and I was okay with that.

My mother, it seems, wasn't.

"So then meet him," the woman who was quickly becoming my ex-best friend said to me from across the table. "What's the worst that can happen?"

"I am pretty sure that every single bad idea in the world started with those words."

I drank the rest of my beer and tried to push the thoughts about Matt from my mind, but they refused to budge. I spent the next few days in a daze as I worked the oncoming Christmas rush, trying to figure out how I could have missed the fact one of the Wallace brothers was gay all this time.

From the time I reached high school, I realized that most of Foster, Texas's school population looked on the Wallace brothers as living legends. They were three of the biggest, strongest, and most athletic guys anyone knew. They always seemed to be together, which gave them the illusion of being bigger than any normal guys I knew, and though no single one of them was stunningly handsome, the three of them together somehow brought their best features out and practically eliminated any weaknesses, so each of them became even better-looking. On the field, they were the very models of a modern-day jock. Off the field, they were an erotic distraction I didn't need.

I remembered Matt was the youngest of the three and the one who made me the most nervous.

When I was a teenager, I had a bad habit of losing my keys, no matter how hard I tried to hold on to them. The space in my brain was finite, and a majority of it was occupied with keeping up my straight pretense, or at least that's how I saw it. Because of that, it was no wonder that other things, like house keys, tended to fall through the cracks.

Sometimes literally.

After the fourth time, my dad refused to make another copy, complaining that there were now more sets of keys to our house wandering around Foster than there were doors to and inside our house. My mother had taken to helping him in the afternoons with the uniform rentals, which meant if I got home and realized I was locked out, I had to wait for someone to come home. It was frustrating at first, but after a while I tried to make the best of it.

I stashed some books under the back porch, and when my keys went missing, I just leaned against the back door and read until someone came home. It was relaxing in a way my teenage mind couldn't process at the time. Being alone was the only time I could be myself, even if it just meant reading a book with my shoes off. I'm not sure when he started doing it, but about a month into my reading, I noticed Matt peeking through my back fence.

At first I had no idea what he was doing there. I would watch him watch me as I waited for him to say something. It took me a few times to realize he was the guy who had been staring at me when I mowed the lawn. I had dismissed it as just another kid staring at the time, but once I connected the two events, I became nervous. Each time he would wander away, leaving me more confused than before. This went on for a week, until the thought that maybe he liked me passed through my mind, which was the worst thing that could have occurred to me. It set off a paranoid set of dominoes that made me wonder if I was giving off some vibe he was picking up on. Those thoughts spiraled into themselves until I headed to my dad's shop and waited for him to close rather than risk being seen as gay.

The sad part was that I never once thought Matt might be gay also.

As I sat in the same shop years later, I felt ancient as I stared at Nancy's Diner across the street. I saw Brad's car pull up in front and him and Kyle jump out and race inside. I had taken an interest in Brad ever since I heard he had come out as Foster High's first gay athlete. Kyle and he had done what I would have never had the guts to do at their age, and the least I could do was try to support them any way I could. Brad was the path not taken, a younger me who hadn't let his fear of being exposed stop him from going after what he really wanted. In Brad's case, that was Kyle.

The two of them looked so happy, so freaking young, that I felt even more depressed. I suppose there is nothing in the world that reminds someone he is an old coot more than seeing a young couple in love. All you can see is the potential, the energy, and the time. They have their whole lives ahead of them.

While mine felt like it was ending one second at a time.

I shook myself out of my self-decorated and catered pity party and decided to take advantage of a rare lull at the shop. I locked the front door and jogged across the street to the diner. It was overrun with the usual lunch crowd, but it wasn't so big a place that I couldn't see where they were sitting from the door.

Out of breath, I slid into the booth and announced, "I need some help." My mouth was dry, and I realized I was so worked up I was close to having a panic attack. I grabbed Brad's Coke and downed it, trying to calm myself.

"Hey," Brad said, scooting over to give me some room. "Um, help yourself."

I nodded as I finished the drink. "Thanks." I looked across the table and smiled. "Hey, Kyle."

Kyle waved back, still half-shocked that I had crashed their date.

"So what's up?" Brad asked, probably wondering if I was having a heart attack or something.

I felt my mind start to lock up as the familiar fear of being found out came back full force. Before I was completely crippled, I blurted out, "My mom is trying to set up me with someone."

Brad looked at me, confused. "Your mom? I thought she lived in Florida."

I heard myself snap at him. "She does, but she still owns a phone." I mentally berated myself immediately—he hadn't done a thing to me. That thought was followed by the humbling fact that I was a grown man talking to two teenagers about my love life because I didn't have any gay friends my own age.

I was truly pathetic.

Brad paused for a moment before asking me in a neutral voice, "Okay, so who is she trying to set you up with?"

"Matt Wallace," I said, picking a piece of ice out of the glass.

"I don't know him. He's from here?" he asked, no doubt curious because he hadn't heard the gay population of Foster had doubled overnight.

"He's from here, but he doesn't live here," I corrected him. "We kind of went to high school together. He lives in San Francisco."

"Your mom is trying to set you up with a guy who lives in another state?" Kyle asked.

I nodded. "Well, he's coming back for Christmas. His parents still live here."

"So she's more setting you up for casual sex," Brad clarified. Kyle and I just gaped at him. "What? It's not like you're going to date him for a week." Neither one of us said a word. "Come *on*! Like I am the only one here who knows what a hookup is."

I shook my head slowly. "I'm pretty sure my mom is not trying to set me up with a hookup." Even though the same thought had crossed my mind a few times.

He shrugged. "Okay, so then what's your problem?"

"I don't know if I should meet him," I said as Gayle brought them their food.

"Oh! Hey, Tyler, you eating?" she asked, surprised to see me sitting with them. Gayle had run Nancy's forever. When I was Brad and Kyle's age, I remembered her working the counter. The only differences between then and now were her hair was a little grayer and there were more lines around her eyes. She seemed like a fixed point that held Foster together. Even though I had never said word one about my sexuality to her, I was pretty sure she knew everything there was to know about my life, sexual preference included.

"I'm not staying that long, but thanks," I said, giving her a smile.

"Okay. Guys, here are your burgers. Holler if you need anything," she called over her shoulder as she walked to another table.

As soon as she was gone, I sighed. "I mean, you're right, I can't date him for a few days. But God, it sucks being gay here." I picked at Brad's plate, eating a fry and making an effort not to get too maudlin.

"Have you tried online?" Kyle asked, putting ketchup on his burger.

"Ugh," I lied, eating another fry. "Complete waste of time."

"So then meet him," Brad offered.

"But what if I like him?" I asked honestly.

"So then don't meet him," Brad suggested, grabbing his burger. I was pretty sure he thought I was going to eat it too.

"But God, Christmas sucks when you're alone." I sighed again. Normally I wouldn't have been this sharing, but it had been a long time since I had other gay people to talk to, even if they were in high school.

"So then meet him, but as a friend," Kyle suggested brightly. "There's nothing saying you have to date or have sex with him. But you can make a new friend and see where that goes."

"Yeah, that's an idea," I agreed between fries. "Actually, a really good idea."

An idea that had never crossed my mind. In my world it was either to fuck or to ignore. There was no in between. The concept of making gay friends... well, it terrified me, so of course it had been the last thing I thought of. "You know? I mean, who said it has to be all or nothing?"

"Well, you did," Kyle countered bluntly. I looked over at him and he added, "You did! All your mom is saying is that there's going to be another gay person in Foster over Christmas. You're the one imbuing it with more importance than it deserves. To be honest, that says more about you than it does about your mom." He had no idea who I was, but I had a growing feeling he knew exactly what my damage was. Linda always bragged about him being special, but I had just passed it off as mother's bragging rights. But he was looking across at me and I could see the wheels turning in his head, and it was kind of frightening. Jokingly I said to Brad, "You date someone this smart? You are a braver man than I am. But you're right. My mom is just trying to be nice, and I completely misread it." I looked at Kyle and decided to test how much he had read off me. So I asked him seriously, "Do I seem that lonely?"

Without a second's hesitation, he answered, "Yes."

Well, that answered my question.

"Yeah. Maybe meeting this guy isn't such a good idea," I said after a while. "If I'm this wound up, I'm just going to mess things up." Looking at Kyle, I grinned. "Good call."

"Thanks," he said, taking a drink of his tea. "Let me ask you something. Why not go out with Robbie?"

I froze, because I always do when I hear that name.

Explaining Robbie would be a lot like picking an infected scab on my arm. It would be excruciating painful, probably do more harm than good, and just make things worse. No one else in town had any idea about the history between us, and we both liked it that way. Also, in explaining Robbie I would have to explain Riley, and to explain Riley would take several bottles of something so strong I'd just be crying by the end of the story.

All of that passed through my mind in a matter of seconds. I knew that none of it was going to come out of my mouth.

So instead I just vauged it up and said, "He isn't my biggest fan. Besides, I don't think we're each other's type."

Kyle leaned forward. "What type is that?"

There were those eyes again. Fuck, this kid was too smart for his own good. "What did he tell you about me?"

"Kyle is working for him," Brad interjected quickly. "At his store."

"Oh," I grunted, knowing he probably knew enough to think I was a complete asshole. "Well then, I'm sure you've heard a lot about me so far." I wanted to ask him how much Robbie had told him when I noticed a couple of people standing in front of my shop peeking in the window. "Dammit, I knew I couldn't leave the store for more than five minutes." I got up. "We've been swamped, and I've had zero time to think about this." I laid a twenty on the table. "That's to make up for me eating all your food." I was about to walk out when a thought hit me. Turning to Brad, I asked, "Hey, you need a job?"

"Me?"

I laughed and pointed to Kyle. "Well, he already has one."

"Um, yeah, I guess," he replied after a few seconds.

"Awesome! Come by after lunch and I'll start training you." I looked at Kyle and then back at Brad. "And you were right, this one is a keeper." I saw Kyle redden slightly as I walked toward the door.

Kyle jumped up. "Mr. Parker, wait!" He hurried over to me. "Can I ask you a question?"

I saw Brad watching us. I nodded. Was this where he told me to fuck off? "Sure, what's up?"

"Have you heard anything about Kelly Aimes?"

Who?

I paused and tried to connect the name with a face. Kelly Aimes sounded familiar, but honestly, a lot of kids went through the shop and I never caught their name. "Which one is he?" I asked.

"Big guy, plays football. Friend of Brad's? Dark hair?" he described.

And suddenly the name clicked for me. Kelly had been Brad's shadow since junior high. Yeah, right—Kelly Aimes—big kid, played good ball. I shook my head. "No, what should I have heard?"

He shook his head. "Nothing. I was just curious."

I was about to press the point when I saw a couple more people walk up to the front of the shop. "Shit. I have to go. Everything okay?" I asked him.

He gave me a pretty good fake smile and nodded. "It's all good, thanks."

It was pretty obvious that "it" was not all good, but I didn't have the time to dwell on Kyle's question. I jogged across the street, and within an hour, all my thoughts consisted of ways to get through the day. In fact, it was a couple of days before I was able to find enough time to hang out with Linda and ask her about it.

"So I had a talk with Kyle," I said over our third beer.

She nodded. "I heard. He asked me how hard it was for you to be that cute and secretly be gay. He couldn't understand how some girl didn't figure it out."

"And what did you say?" I asked, knowing she was setting me up.

"I told him some girl did figure it out. Me." She gave me a bratty smile, and I stuck my tongue out at her. "So, you make a decision on the Wallace boy yet?"

"Your son seems of the opinion that I am overthinking it," I commented between sips.

She chuckled. "My son seems to have nailed the problem in one. Admit it, he has, hasn't he?"

I grumbled before I finished my beer. "He might have a small point."

"Oh no! He is completely, one hundred percent correct, and you know it." She sounded so smug, it killed me, because she was right. I hated it when she was right because it usually meant I was wrong since we didn't agree on much. "Look, Tyler, we both know why you're shy about meeting people, but that was then, this is now."

Of course Linda knew about everything that had gone down, but it wasn't something we talked about. And she was right; I was gun-shy about meeting other gay people that weren't specifically being met to fuck and leave. Just the thought of meeting this guy had put me into a downward spiral I hadn't felt since....

Well, since Riley was killed.

"I'm fine," I said, trying to make it sound as truthful as possible.

She laughed. "You have never, in your entire life, been fine. In fact if fine walked right up to you and introduced itself, you'd have no fucking idea what to say."

I asked her sarcastically, "Have I informed you lately that I hate you?"

She shrugged. "It's a given."

I nodded as we finished our beer.

"So Kyle quit his job," she said in the gap.

That got my attention. "The one with Robbie?" I asked, trying not to seem too interested.

"Yes, that one." She rolled her eyes. "Probably for the best, I mean, you know how he is."

I did, but she really didn't. Linda disliked Robbie simply because she was my friend. I loved her for that, but it really didn't make her an impartial judge.

"Did he say why?"

"No, and I didn't ask."

I left it at that. Last thing I needed was Robbie in my mind.

I WENT home, buzzed as always, and fell into bed.

The house was quiet, as it always was. My parents had bought this house after they were married and knew they were going to have kids, so they made sure it was huge. It turns out that after me they gave up on that idea, which left me an only child.

The house was fine growing up, but since they moved it had been just me, and let me tell you, I never felt more alone than in this house. It was like it knew it was being wasted. The very walls told me I was wasting its potential, that I was never going to marry or have kids, so why was I here?

Why was I here?

I drifted off, and as always, my mind went back to the past, the past I had been running from for a while now.

I had just gotten done with physical therapy and had been helping my dad out at the shop, slowly learning how to run it for my eventual takeover, when someone I knew walked in. Foster was a small town, so everyone knew everyone a little, but Riley Mathison was one of those people everyone knew.

His family was richer than God, most of the town had been built by them, and though they were rarely seen, everyone knew who they were. They had two daughters, complete demons from what I heard, went to private school, never interacted with Foster at all, so an unknown.

The story was that they thought they could do better for Riley by having him go to school in town, you know, to socialize with us commoners.

Well, Riley was nothing like his sisters. He was kind, sincere, and of course handsome as all hell. He was a fairy-tale prince who seemed too good to be true. He went to Foster and played sports, of course, so I knew him only as a rival. I had crushed on him; who hadn't? He seemed perfect from the outside.

I hadn't thought much about him since high school, and seeing him walk in was like suddenly being thrown back in time.

He didn't seem to notice me behind the counter at first, but as he came down one of the aisles, he looked up, saw me, and paused. He seemed confused for a moment, and then he smiled at me. "Tyler, right?"

I nodded as my mouth went dry. He remembered me?

"Riley Mathison, we played football at the same time."

Like anyone would forget who he was.

"What's up, man?" I asked, trying to be casual.

"Not much. I just got married and moved back into town. You?"

Of course he was married, to some lucky fucking girl who he screwed every night.

"Just helping my dad out," I said, trying not to sound bitter.

"I heard what happened to your knee, man. That's rough."

I nodded, not wanting to talk about any of this.

"So, who's the lucky girl?" I asked. "Someone from here?"

He paused. "It's a guy. I'm gay."

I literally just froze. The only sound was the blood rushing to my ears. What had he just said? Was he serious? Was this one of those jokes where they scream "psych" and then laugh at the look on your face? Why was he saying it? Did he know about me? Was this a test? Was this a trap? Fuck.

His face darkened a little. "No big deal, just wanted to say hey." He thought I was upset, he thought I was disgusted…. He thought I was everyone else.

I saw him turn to walk away, and I had to make a choice, take off my mask and reveal my secret identity or just let him walk out.

"Riley, wait!"

He paused and turned back to look at me.

I looked around to make sure no one else was near. My heart felt like it was about to explode. I hadn't told another living soul outside of Linda and my parents, and now I was going to tell a stranger? A guy I spoke five words to in high school?

Was I?

"Yeah?" he asked, probably thinking I was going to spit on him or something.

"Um, me too."

He cocked his head. "You too what?"

"I'm too."

"Tyler, what are you—"

"I'm gay!"

And there it is, ladies and gentlemen. You can clock it. Tyler Parker admitted he was gay for the first time at the ripe old age of twenty-five.

"Shut up," he said, moving back to the counter.

This was it. I could say it was a joke and move on. All I had to do was lie.

"I am," my mouth said, completely independent of my brain.

"Since when?"

I almost said since now, but that wasn't true. I thought about it for a moment.

"Since forever I guess. I mean, I had a feeling, but I knew it in high school for sure."

"Holy shit," he marveled. "Tyler Parker is gay?"

I laughed. "Riley Mathison is gay?"

"We do seem to be the least likely guys in Foster to be queer, huh?"

I nodded, and I felt a little dizzy. My head was light, and I had this feeling like I was drunk. It took me a second to realize the feeling of this massive weight bearing down on me had been lifted… and I had no idea how to handle that.

"So, you single?" he asked.

"Of course, who would I date around here?"

"There are a lot of guys out at the Bear's Den."

I made a face. "That gay bar outside of town? Why the hell would I go there?"

"Um, because you're gay, stupid."

It's funny, when he said it like that, it sounded so logical.

"Look," he said grabbing a piece of paper and a pen from the counter. "This is our address. Come by, meet my husband, and we'll talk more."

He handed me the paper and I just stared at it, not moving to take it.

He put it down on the counter. "It's up to you, man. But if you want some gay friends, you know where to find us."

I nodded, not sure about anything at all.

He walked out, and I watched him go. I looked down at the paper and then back up to see him cross the street.

And suddenly it was night and we were outside the Bear's Den. A truck came screaming by and hit him, throwing him up into the air.

I WOKE up screaming.

I was covered in sweat, and my sheets were thrown all over the bed. I sat up and tried to breathe, but my chest was tight with terror. Fuck, I hadn't had that dream in forever. That had happened years and years ago, but it felt like yesterday. I got up and turned the shower on. As I waited for it to warm up, I looked at myself in the mirror and did not like who I saw looking back at me.

I knew I was good-looking; that wasn't me bragging, it was a statement of fact. The majority of people who saw me found me more attractive than most other people. I took pride in it, sure, but I also hated it.

I knew what I looked like. Dirty blond hair, blue eyes, white teeth, easy smile. I was the fucking poster boy of normalcy. If Texas was going to run an ad campaign about how wholesome Texas boys are, I would be its face. They'd have me in a tight pair of Wranglers, buttoned-up shirt, hat…. I'd look at the camera, wink, and say, "Y'all are always welcome here." Girls would swoon, guys would raise an eyebrow, and the whole world would go, "See, that's a nice boy." There would only be two people in world who would know the truth: that I was a complete piece of shit and one of the ugliest people alive.

Robbie and I, we'd know.

THE NEXT week consisted of a blur of people coming in and out, buying every sports-related present they could think of. Oh, and occasional food and less-occasional sleep. Even with Brad's help, I was overwhelmed by the amount of foot traffic walking in empty-handed and staggering out with at least one piece of equipment or clothing in a bag. The only good thing about that was I had little time to think about Matt and what I wanted to do about him. In fact, I had almost forgotten him entirely in the haze of exhaustion the Christmas rush created.

Then I got a call from Linda late one afternoon.

"Is this my monthly call from Dial-a-Bitch?" I asked, tossing a load of uniforms into the washing machine. Brad was out front dealing with customers while I tried to catch up with all the back work we had.

"He's here" was all she said.

"Who?" I asked jokingly. "Jesus? Does he look pissed? Does he still have those abs?"

Her voice got even sterner, which was saying something about Linda's voice. "Matt. Wallace. Is. Here," she whispered into the phone. She was at work, which meant she was using her cell at the register, something she could get fired for.

I felt my stomach clench up.

"He just walked in the door. If you want to run into him casual-like instead of being hooked up by your mother, then you better haul ass down here." She hung up, leaving me standing there dumbfounded, staring blankly at my phone.

Part of me wanted to run out the door; the other part wanted to never leave this building until he left town. A million things ran through my mind at once. What if I liked him? What if I didn't? What if he told everyone about me? What if I pissed him off and he threatened to expose me? What if....

I glanced out at the store and saw Kyle had brought Brad lunch from Nancy's. They were so fucking cute it was criminal. Kyle was feeding Brad fries one at a time; Brad leaned over the counter, snapping at the food as Kyle pulled it away. My chest actually ached, I wanted something like that so much. I wanted someone to bring me lunch, to tease me, to make me laugh... I wanted....

I dropped the uniforms and rushed through the front of the shop. "He's here," I yelled at Brad and Kyle as I passed them. "Lock up for me!" I'm not sure if they understood what I said, but I trusted them to handle the shop in my absence.

The Best Buy was just on the edge of town, part of the new shopping complex they opened up a few years ago. It seems a development company came into town wanting to build one of those gigantic mega mall complexes with the Best Buy as the corner store. The city council had turned down their request to build it off Second Street, saying it would have disrupted the flow of the city proper. I didn't know what they meant by that, but I assumed it was something along the lines of "We don't like change!" so the idea went away, but the mall didn't. The parking lot was crowded as usual this time of the year, but "crowded" for Foster is probably like a Tuesday anywhere else. I rushed past the Toys for Tots Marine just inside the front door, doing my level best to ignore the hot uniformed man who was way too young for me to be looking at.

I glanced over at her usual register and saw Linda pointing to the back of store by the games. Nodding, I moved as fast as possible without breaking into a run, slowing down slightly to grab a few DVDs on the way. The electronics section was at the back of Best Buy in a quiet corner—well, relatively quiet corner. A dead-end department, it was designed to give buyers nowhere else to go once they'd stepped in its trap. From the looks of things, a bunch of people had stepped in at the same time. I scanned up and down the aisles for him, even standing on tiptoe once in an effort to see someone familiar. At the same time, I racked my brain to remember what he looked like. I had seen a recent pic on the website he worked for, but a picture and the real thing can be vastly different. I must have looked like a lost kid searching for my parents standing in the middle of the video games aisle.

And then I saw him walking away from me.

I held my breath, not sure what to do next. Should I just let him walk away? Would I not say a word and let the opportunity slip away? From what I could see, he was still in great shape. He turned his head to look at something and I saw his profile. He was as handsome as ever. I was so anxious I felt myself start to sweat....

"Matt!" my mouth called out against my will. *What the fuck, mouth?* I asked myself. *Not like you were going to make a move, chicken,* my mind answered back as Matt turned to look at me.

"Now we're in it," I mumbled under my breath.

My Judas mind said nothing, but I could hear it chuckle as I walked toward him.

MATT

"IT's ME," he said as if someone could have forgotten him even for a second. "Tyler? Tyler Parker?"

"Tyler," I echoed. Like a robot president at Disneyland, I suddenly came to life and shook his hand. "I'm Matt," I added.

Our hands paused in midshake, and he replied, "I know. I just said it, like, three times."

I kicked myself mentally as I nodded. "Right, just seeing if you were paying attention." And then kicked myself harder. My brain laughed uproariously.

He half laughed and half made a sound that might have been "Uh-huh" before he released my hand, which I'd forgotten about. Handshake... oh yeah. Handshake. "How weird seeing you here, huh?" he asked as dazed, Christmas-numb people milled around us.

"Right?" I said. I wasn't sure what language was coming out of my mouth, but I was pretty certain it wasn't English. "What are you doing here?"

He grinned as if waiting for me to add a "Just kidding" on the end of my statement. When he realized it wasn't coming, he answered, "I live here. What about you? Kinda far from California, aren't you?"

"You know where I live?" I asked, the dumbfounded look on my face returning.

"It's a small town." He chuckled. "And not many people get out and stay out, so yeah, I heard you had moved."

"Yeah. I moved to California," I said and went back to kicking myself. My mind, traitor that it was, continued guffawing.

He burst out laughing. "Well, to answer your question more accurately, I'm trying to get someone to help me, but I think I'm SOL," he said while looking around for an employee to corner.

How anyone could not drop what they were doing to come running to help him was beyond me. "You buying a gift?" I asked in what may have been the first normal thing I'd uttered since I'd seen him. He had some DVDs in his hand, so it was a fair guess.

"I wish," he said, running a hand through his hair as he looked around in apprehension. "My computer committed suicide this week, and I did everything I know to get it working again. So I'm kinda forced to buy a new one."

"How old is it?" I asked, suddenly in a world I could actually form coherent sentences about.

He paused for a moment, trying to remember. "Less than two years, but you know how computers are today." Abruptly, he stopped and looked at me. "What am I saying? Of course you know how computers are, my bad."

"You know what I do for a living?" I asked, once again shocked.

He blushed a little more. "Guilty, I've read your column a couple of times. You're pretty funny."

I was pretty sure I was on the floor of Best Buy, body twitching in the throes of a brain-damaging embolism, but as fantasies went, this one was nice.

"So, yeah," he continued, jamming his hands in his pockets and looking around again. "But at this point I'm better off just chucking a dart and buying whatever it lands on."

"I can look at it," I blurted out before my internal filter could stop me. *What the hell?* my inner self asked me silently. *Oh, you were never going to make a move*, I retorted. *Fuck off.*

Aloud I added, "I mean, if it's that new, I'm sure it is just a power supply or maybe the hard drive. Both of those can be replaced for a lot less than a whole new system."

I was praying I didn't sound as desperate as I did in my own ears.

"Really?" he asked, shocked. "You'd do that?"

I tried to play it casual. "Of course. I mean, what are friends for?"

He looked at me for several seconds, and I wondered if he was going to point out that we had never actually been friends. "I mean, I know you're down here for Christmas, and I don't want to take you away from—"

"Please!" I exclaimed. "Take me away from them!" And we both laughed. "It wouldn't be a problem at all, honestly."

"Okay then, if you're sure," he said again. I almost said, "I'd consider hitting my mother on the back of the head with a snow shovel if kissing you was in the cards." But I thought that would come off as needy.

"I'm sure," I answered.

"You remember where I live?" he asked.

"You still live there?" Now I wondered if he had seen me stalking him earlier. "My parents moved to Florida a couple of years ago, and they gave it to me. Never had the heart to sell it."

"Yeah, I remember. Where you live, I mean," I said after pretending I had to search my memory.

"Awesome!" Tyler's face lit up, causing my knees to grow weak. "When is good for you?"

I forced myself not to say *now* and instead offered, "How about tomorrow?"

He pulled a business card out of his wallet and handed it to me. "That has my cell on it. Call me and let me know when you're heading over, all right?"

He gave me that three-second stare again and then laughed. "Okay! Well, awesome. Thanks for this, Matt. I owe you one. Uh, I'm going to go pay for these," he said, holding up a handful of movies. I could see from the spines they were two animated movies and the latest sci-fi thriller.

"Those are great movies!" I exclaimed.

He looked down and nodded. "Yeah, I saw them in the theater, just never got around to picking them up on DVD." He looked up and asked earnestly, "You sure this isn't a problem?"

"Nah," I said, trying not to imagine the different ways he could repay me. "It's Christmas, after all."

"Tomorrow, then?" We shook hands again, maybe holding on a little longer than was strictly necessary.

"Count on it," I said, this time savoring the physical contact and really taking a second to soak in what I could see of him. Though I was a year younger than Tyler, he was in excellent shape, better than I was if I could tell by the button-up shirt and khakis he wore. He looked like a television model come to life. His teeth were perfect, and I could see a light dusting of freckles on his face that made me want to stare even more than I suddenly realized I was.

He smiled before he turned and walked away, and I had to admit he was as hot going as he had been coming.

I was in a daze by the time I got home. I resisted the urge to drive by his house to somehow verify he had been telling the truth and that the past two hours hadn't been the culmination of a decade-long joke where I get my heart broken at the end.

Instead, I drove sedately to my parents' house, packed the new system into my brother's trunk, and walked back into the house as if nothing had happened.

Things had calmed down some; the smaller kids had been put to bed, and my brothers and dad sat around the TV watching what looked like one of the Marvel movies while the older kids sat on the floor transfixed by the special effects. My mother was at the dining room table with the wives. She got up as soon as she saw me. "You were gone awhile. I was worried," she said, grabbing my hands. "Come sit with us." She tried to pull me toward the table.

It was bad enough that I was treated like a stranger every year because I'd had the nerve to leave the town and stay gone, but for some reason, being consigned to the women's table was just too much for me. "I'm fine, Mom. I think I'm going to wash up and get ready for bed."

"Oh," she said, trying to hide being upset. "Well, I wanted to talk to you about Frances's son because—"

And something snapped.

"Look, Mom," I said, trying to keep my voice down. "I am not alone. I am not lonely. I am not miserable, and I do not need my mother trying to hook me up with men on Christmas, okay?" She looked as if I had slapped her. "I just…." I tried to compose myself. "I just don't want to talk about this with you, please."

Her face hardened as she tried to hide the pain. "Well, fine," she said, turning back to the table. "Fresh towels are in the closet," she added. As if I hadn't lived here for eighteen years. I looked around and saw that everyone was staring at me as if I had decided to defecate in the middle of the living room. They were clearly disgusted.

"I hate Christmas," I said, taking the stairs two at a time and fleeing toward the shower.

TYLER

I RANG up the movies at Linda's register. "So, you're a big cartoon lover now?" she said, scanning them in.

"Shut up," I snarled at her, looking around as subtly as I could without looking like I was looking. "They were the first things I saw."

"Oh, and look!" she chirped brightly. "*Starship Troopers*. Didn't this win an Oscar or something?"

"You're loving this, aren't you?" I groaned, seeing the glee in her face as she bagged the movies.

"Oh, in so many ways!" She smiled back. "But you talked to him! That is a huge event for you. I'm proud." I searched her face for signs of a dig, but I saw the sincerity in her eyes. "I mean it, three points for just showing up."

I cocked my head. "Three? Are we playing basketball now?"

She pushed the bag of movies at me. "Shut up. I know those games have points and balls; past that I couldn't care."

I slid them back to her. "Keep them, give them to Kyle or Toys for Tots or something. We both know I'm not going to watch them."

She put them behind her counter. "So, what are you going to do now?"

I pulled my keys out of my pocket and grinned at her. "Find a way to break my computer that seems legit."

She looked confused for a moment.

"I made up a story about my laptop being broken so he could come by and fix it."

She gave me a grin. "That sounds like it's right out of a sitcom."

"I had to think fast!"

"Not your specialty," she teased.

"Anyways, I need to find a way to break it without, you know, actually breaking it."

"Also," she added as I walked away, "you might want to clear your browsing history."

I wanted to say something snarky back at her, but I didn't because she was right—again—and I hadn't thought of that.

MATT

THE NEXT morning, I got up early hoping to catch a moment to myself before the insanity began. I made my way downstairs and went straight for the smell of coffee. My father sat at the kitchen table, coffee mug in one hand, folded paper in the other. I thought about sneaking back upstairs, because the only thing worse than dealing with my family en masse was dealing with my father by himself.

"Coffee's hot," he said, not looking up. "Better get it before it's gone."

"Busted," I muttered under my breath, sounding more like a seven-year-old than anything. A row of mugs sat on the counter next to the coffee brewer. I picked up the old green-and-blue plaid one with my name on it and poured myself a cup of coffee. My father didn't move, but I knew he'd already told me to sit down without saying a word. I sat across from him and slid the business section out from the stack, hoping we could skip the lecture for once and just sit there in silence.

"We're not stupid, you know," he said from behind his paper.

No luck.

"I never said you were, Dad." I sighed as I put the paper down.

He put down his paper and looked across at me. I had always shrunk from his stare, even as a little boy. It was as if I knew from an early age I was going to be the one who broke the mold. Two perfect little jock boys for Dad, and then there was me. We had never talked about it openly, but as an adult, I still couldn't imagine I was anything but a failed son or, worse, a twisted daughter to him. That thought killed me a little more every time I had it.

"You act like we are," he said, as if he was Chuck Heston speaking from the top of Mount Sinai holding two stone tablets that both said "Thou shalt not be gay" on them. "You're short with us, and the sighing and the eye rolling makes you look like you're still nine. I don't know if you even realize you're doing it, but it's offensive."

I was shocked because I had thought I had a better poker face than that. "I didn't, I mean, I never meant to…."

He waved his hand, indicating he wasn't done. "You aren't as smart as you think, Matt. Oh, you're smart enough to fool yourself, and that's always been your problem."

This wasn't the annual Christmas scolding I normally got; worse, this wasn't about me snapping at my mom. This was something altogether different. At a loss and floundering, I asked, "Meaning what?"

"Meaning this," he said, putting his coffee down and staring me straight in the eye. "Are you happy?"

"Yes," I answered too quickly.

"No, don't just answer. Think on it and *then* answer. Are you happy, Matt? I mean, you hated this town so much, you took off the second they put a diploma in your hand. I couldn't figure out if you left because of the town or because of us, but I didn't say anything. You said you couldn't be you here, and that was fine. If you were going to be out there and happy, I was fine with that. But it's going on ten years, Matt, and you're still as miserable as the day you left this house. So I ask you again, are you happy?"

This was the most my dad had spoken to me all at once in—well, ever. Normally my mom was the one who spoke for the family, and I assumed she did because my dad never really wanted to deal with me. But this was a level of insight that frankly was beyond my mom. I was stunned into silence. Evidently I had been wrong about that and, from the sound of things, a lot more as far as my father was concerned. His insight came from a perspective my mom could never have, and it hit me hard.

"Because if being gay and being here makes you miserable? I can understand that." He stood and grabbed his red-striped Christmas mug. "But if you're gay there and still that sad, have you considered your being sad has nothing to do with Foster at all?"

He walked out of the kitchen, neatly avoiding my nephews, who came bounding down the stairs, followed by their weary mothers, who no doubt *loved* Christmas break as much as I did. Within twenty minutes the house was bustling with activity and my dad was back to being my dad again, but his words stung like nothing I'd ever felt before.

"So, we're going to throw the ball around," John said, slapping my back. "You coming with us so we can kick your ass?"

Normally I would have joined in, at the very least to rub it in my brothers' faces that at least one of us still possessed a waistline. But Dad's words had left me numb, and there was Tyler....

I felt a slight thrill knowing I had talked with him, in real life and not some hormone-induced coma.

"I actually have to go help a friend fix his computer today," I said, shaking my head. "Maybe later."

"You have friends here?" he asked with a goofy grin. "When did that happen, 'cause I know you didn't have any when you lived here." He burst out laughing as he walked away, no doubt to share his new joke with the rest of the family.

I would have told him to fuck off if he hadn't been right.

I had stayed in contact with absolutely no one when I left town, since I believed everyone I actually knew only tolerated me because they were friends of my brothers. I'm sure my silence only helped my reputation of being stuck-up, but I didn't really care at the time. Now I wondered what I was pulling away from in high school—in fact, in my whole life.

The funny thing was that, looking back, Tyler was the same type of guy I was. Though he had friends, I had heard more than once he was aloof, remote, even cold to most people. Of course, back then he could do no wrong, so I'd ignored the stories, but as I thought about it now, it made perfect sense.

We were both afraid and hiding in our own skins.

After breakfast, I grabbed my laptop, slipped it into my bag, and told my mom I'd be back before dinner. She was still mad and barely grunted as she helped my sisters-in-law make lunch for when the boys would be back. If there was anyone on earth capable of feeding a grudge longer than I could, it was my mom.

It was going to be a long Christmas.

I decided to walk. The weather was decent, and fresh air invigorated me when I inhaled. The truth, of course, was that I hadn't had an excuse for years to approach Tyler's house on foot, and I had never had a solid reason. Now I had both. Another deep breath in the silence of the morning and I walked down to the sidewalk.

It was like a time warp; with each step, I felt like I was being hypnotized. The noise of my shoes hitting the pavement drew me back, and I could feel my thoughts going rewinding. I felt like I'd stumbled into a slipstream. Every step was another bit of time back toward the point where I'd first approached his house, hoping to see him. I couldn't remember the last time I was really happy, and it was bugging me. I had been satisfied and I had been content, but actually being happy had always eluded me. On that quiet walk, I faced the facts. I had been deferring actual happiness to some future point that was never going to come.

I'd be happy when I moved out of Foster. I'd be happy once I graduated college. I'd be happy when I had a career instead of a job. I'd be happy—when? It ceased being a statement and began being a question I knew I still couldn't answer.

I kept pushing it off to later, and now it was later and nothing had changed. I wasn't happy in California; even I could admit that. I thought that being openly gay would suddenly solve all my problems. Like there was a place you go and sign up. You hand them your straight card and they give you a gift basket with ABBA's greatest hits, some lube, and an eight-pack of condoms and say welcome to the neighborhood. Then you would grow up, meet the perfect guy, and just…

Wow, I had no idea what happy would look like past that point.

Deep in thought though I was, I still stopped walking at the head of the Parker sidewalk. Another deep breath, a sharp right turn, and I traveled the few feet from the road to his porch on autopilot.

I knocked on the front door. When would I be happy? Was I even capable of it? Maybe I was just a naturally miserable person, destined to be alone. I didn't know what was worse—not knowing the answer or knowing it and not wanting to accept it. I knocked again and checked my watch, a little thread of anxiety winding through me. It was almost noon, so I knew I wasn't too early.

The door swung open, and I almost fell off the porch.

He was standing there, hair wet, a blue towel clutched around his waist. If I had thought he was in good shape before, I was assured by the way the water dripped off each and every muscle. "What? Oh…," he said, once he realized it was me. "You didn't call."

"What?" I echoed, noticing the way the wet towel bulged and then unable to look away.

"I was expecting you to call," he said, sounding more shocked than angry. "I was in the shower. Come on in and have a seat," he added, moving aside. "Make yourself at home. I'll be right down." I watched him climb the stairs and realized that sixteen-year-old me would have blown his load right then and there. I was relieved I had a bit more control. To keep my attention off Tyler's attributes, I looked around the part of the house I could see from the living room couch. Of course, thinking of the word couch and what a person could do with another person on said couch caused a near misfire, so I firmly fixed my attention on the furniture and pictures around me.

The house was comfortable; it looked like a family still lived here instead of just him. I looked around for signs of a wife or kids, but all I saw were pictures of him in high school and college. There was one of him, on one knee in his football jersey and pads, that transfixed me. He was so young, so flawless; it was the very image I had fallen in love with years ago. His smile was wide, and his pride at the moment radiated from the past, like heat from a flame.

"That was sophomore year," he said from behind me. "My first year on the team, I thought I was the shit."

He was pulling on a T-shirt when I turned around. His flat stomach should have been illegal, I thought as I casually continued my stare past him, taking in the rest of the room. "My brothers were on the team before me, so for me, my first year felt like going into the family business." I discovered that feigning casualness could end up with me staring at a closet door. Still casual, I swung my gaze back around to focus on him.

He chuckled. "Yeah, you guys were kinda legendary around here." He gestured to the den. "It's in there. D'you want something to drink?"

"I'm good," I said, following him. He was barefoot, and I was instantly reminded of catching him reading in the backyard. I felt my body begin to react as he led me to a decent laptop; it looked fine from the outside. "Here she is. Finicky bitch, if you ask me."

"Huh?" I asked, his words not making sense for a moment. "Oh right, the computer." I covered quickly. "Lemme take a look."

He kept on talking while I booted it up to see what would happen. "So, I saw the cars in front of your house. Christmas must be insane over there."

I nodded as I scanned the bios and bootup process. "I always offer to get a room out at the Motel 8, but my mom takes mortal offense for some reason." It looked fine, but it wasn't starting Windows.

"Yeah. I'm an only child, always wondered what a big family would have been like," he mused.

"Complicated," I answered, sighing when I thought of my mom. I checked a few more things and then turned it off. "Okay, looks like it can't find Windows. Might be your hard drive."

"That bad?" he asked as if we were talking about a sick child.

I laughed and pulled my laptop out. "Nah, I'm going to take yours and hook it up to here as a second drive. That way I can look at its directory."

He blinked a few times. "All I know is I push that button and the computer turns on."

I laughed. "Okay, works for me. Seriously, it doesn't look bad." I took out a set of cables from my bag and started to pop the back off it. "So, I'm surprised you moved back to town. Didn't you get a scholarship for football or something?"

"Florida," he confirmed. "And yeah, blew my knee out second year and had to drop out."

I stopped and looked back at him. "Man, I'm sorry. I know you loved the game."

He nodded and looked down for a second. "It took some time, but I got over it."

I might have been imagining it, but he didn't sound too sure about the "getting over" part.

"Well, you look great," I said before realizing what I'd just said. "I mean, you walk fine." Even worse. "I mean, no limp." I went back to the laptop.

"Thanks," he said wryly. "So did you bring anyone home for Christmas?"

"No, I'm single," I said and then realized what he had asked. "I mean, I'm not seeing anyone to bring home, and even if I was, I don't doubt I'd scare them away by introducing them to my family. I mean a girl, introduce a girl to."

"Dude, I know you're gay," he interrupted quietly, out of nowhere.

My hands went numb, and I froze in place.

"It's cool, seriously," he added. "I kinda am too," he said, his voice trailing off.

I turned around slowly, pretty sure I was still having that stroke. "You?" I said pointing.

"Yeah, me," he said a little defensively. "Why? You get to be the only gay guy in town?"

"Mr. Sanders is gay," I said, still in shock.

"The florist?" he exclaimed and then shook. "Brrr, that guy is a major perv."

I just stared with my mouth open.

"Why do you look so shocked?" he finally asked.

I went back to the computer. "I just never suspected. I mean, you were the last person I'd ever thought of being gay too."

"How can you say that? You didn't even know me," he challenged.

"I knew of you," I said, trying to remember that the boy I had in my mind was in no way the man in front of me.

"Besides peeking through my back fence, which doesn't count as talking, when did you ever talk to me?" My head whipped around, and he laughed. "Oh yeah, I noticed you watching me. Er, it was kinda hard not to."

"Why didn't you say anything?" I asked, feeling like my entire life had been a lie.

He shrugged. "'Cause I didn't want to admit I liked guys back then. Still don't, to be honest. But back then, serious closet case."

We both sat there in stunned silence. Finally I said, "Can you imagine if we'd known about each other back in high school?"

He laughed. "There's a baseball player at Foster High who just came out. Has a boyfriend and everything."

"No shit?" I asked, not believing it. "And everyone is okay with it?"

"They aren't okay with it, but what are they going to do, lynch them? They're in love, and most people respect that."

"I think my brothers would have exploded if I'd come out while I was playing ball," I admitted.

"Yeah, my dad almost had a heart attack," he said, rubbing his hands on his pants. "You need a beer?"

I hated beer, but I did need a drink. "Please."

"Great," he said, jumping up and heading to the kitchen.

As I attached his laptop to mine and started running a diagnostic, I wondered how different things would have been if we both had known we liked guys back then. Would we have been different people? Would we be happy? Would it have mattered?

"Here," he said from behind me.

I straightened and turned to take the bottle, and he kissed me. I can't imagine it was pleasurable for him at first, since I didn't even breathe as I felt his arm go around my waist and pull me closer. Whatever shock had paralyzed me wore off fast, though, as I melted into his arms and kissed him back properly.

My head spun as I felt our tongues move past each other. Years of dreaming and desire reached fruition in one instant. The kiss ended, but our heads stayed touching as he whispered, "I'm sorry. I've wanted to do that since I saw you at the store."

"I've been wanting you to do that since I saw you reading in the backyard," I admitted.

I saw the glow of his teeth as he grinned at me. "Really?"

I nodded silently, unsure if I could trust my mouth to say the right thing or not.

"You wanna keep kissing or you wanna work on the computer?" he asked.

"Can we do both?" I asked hopefully.

He barked out a laugh. "Dude, I'm happy with both."

I pulled back and tried to catch my breath. "Let me fix the computer first."

He shook his head as he fell back into the oversized chair across from me. One of his feet dangled over an arm, and I forced myself not to watch him open his beer. "All work and no play…," he teased.

"The sooner I fix this, the sooner I can get payment," I said, giving him an evil smile back.

I began accessing his hard drive, not believing what was happening. "So, a baseball player?" I said as I typed. "I can't even imagine coming out like that."

"Yeah, that's what I thought too, but he has a guy and they're dating… the whole nine yards," Tyler said as he took a sip of his beer. "I mean, it hasn't been in the paper or anything, but it's pretty common knowledge around town."

I paused. "Am I common knowledge?" I dared to ask.

He shook his head. "No. I've never heard about you in the Foster Gay Underground," he said with a smile.

"There's, like, what? Four of you sitting around at the Veteran's club on folding chairs talking about people they heard were gay?" I asked, shaking my head.

"There're six of us, thank you, and we couldn't book the Veteran's club. The lesbians took it before us." I had to laugh with him at that. "So what's San Francisco like?" he asked after a while. "I bet you're a popular boy there."

"I said I was single, didn't I?"

"Yeah, but that's 'cause you're playing the market, right?" he offered. "I've thought about selling the house and moving out there a couple of times."

"Why didn't you?" I asked.

He shrugged and finished his beer. "Don't know, never had the guts to do it."

"You'd be the belle of the ball," I said, going back to my laptop.

"Oh really?" he asked suggestively. "And why is that?"

"You have to know you're incredibly good-looking," I said, not daring to look into his eyes. "You can have any guy you want."

"And if I want you?" he asked bluntly.

I blushed as I typed for a few seconds on my laptop. "Found your problem," I said.

"Too aggressive?" he asked.

"I meant with your laptop. Can I ask you a question?"

He nodded.

"Did you disconnect the hard drive on purpose to get me over here?"

He said nothing, but I saw him blush.

"Oh my God, you did!"

"How was I supposed to get you over here? Just blurt out in the middle of Best Buy I'm gay and want to meet you?"

"Um, yes?"

He laughed. "Yeah, I couldn't do that."

I reconnected his hard drive, closed up the laptop, and turned it on.

"Good as before you broke it," I said with a smile.

"It was kind of stupid, right?"

"Yeah, you could have actually broken it…."

"I wasn't talking about the computer, dummy," he said, grabbing my shirt and pulling me to my feet as he kissed me again. This time I was ready and kissed him back. We stood there for almost ten minutes, our hands roaming everywhere as we savagely kissed each other. As my hand coasted down to his jeans, I was pleasantly surprised to find the bulge that had been visible behind the towel was prominent. My knees threatened to melt under me, and I couldn't have cared less.

"You're still hot," I said as we caught our breath.

"I always had a crush on your family," he admitted. "The three of you were like sex in sneakers walking down the road."

"I'm sure you were more turned on by my brothers," I said softly.

His hand pulled my chin up as we made eye contact. "Your brothers aren't here with me," he said in a deep voice. "And I'm glad they aren't."

"So am I," I said as my laptop chirped.

"You're beeping," he said between kisses.

"Let it beep," I said as we fell back onto the couch.

TYLER

TEN YEARS ago, I would have mounted him right there on the couch.

Five years ago, there would have been ten minutes of making out before we were naked.

Now we just lay on the couch and enjoyed the feel of each other's body as we talked. I was horned up, but just feeling him lying on top of me felt so nice, so calming, I could have fallen asleep if we hadn't been talking. We kissed a few times—okay, more than a few—but we also began asking each other what our lives were like. We hadn't been friends in high school, but high school had ended a long time ago; we were comfortable with each other, feeling we had always known each other in some way.

Maybe I was just that lonely, maybe I was that starved for physical attention, but the feeling was a thousand times more intimate than sex ever had been. A whole slew of thoughts that scared the shit out of me raced through my mind as we talked. Like how perfect he felt there in my arms, or how I could lie there on the couch with him forever, if that were a choice. I didn't care if someone found out about us or if he told anyone. Those fears were gone for the moment, and I had to admit, the silence in my mind was addictive.

I bring this up because I won't mention it later to Matt, which will be a mistake. I mention it now to you because it will literally be the only record of what I felt like in the moment. I say this now in plain, old-fashioned English because not saying it later will be part of the bigger problem.

I was happy, and it was a feeling I wanted a lot more of.

I now leave you to our story, already in progress.

MATT

WE LAY in each other's arms on the couch, enjoying the feel of each other in a way that sixteen-year-old me would have never believed. His finger stroked my triceps as he was telling me about getting his knee ruined during a game. "I remember lying there on the field thinking, 'This is the end of my life.' Looking back, I don't even remember the pain, even when they put me on the gurney to roll me off; all I knew was that I was never going to play again."

"That must have been horrible," I said, empathizing with him as I saw football through his eyes. The game had always been something I had to do to keep people off my trail, so I never liked it the way my brothers had. But hearing Tyler talk about his accident and the literal bone-crushing injury of not being able to play again, I felt a shiver at the base of my spine.

He was quiet for a moment and then shrugged. "You know, when I was in the locker room and they were inspecting my leg, I remember thinking my dad was going to be so disappointed." His voice got rough, and he stopped talking for a few seconds. "Anyway, you don't want to hear my sob story."

I moved up and leaned in to kiss him. "Hey, I want to hear all your stories. Sob and otherwise."

He smiled back. "Oh really?"

I nodded, kissing him again. "Every single one."

"What about you?" he asked after a few kisses.

"What about me?" I asked, settling back down on his chest. "I went to college, moved to the city, and review tech things. That's my story."

"You sound thrilled," he said, rubbing my back in long, easy strokes that evolved into circles, still calming. I almost purred, which would have been embarrassing.

"I thought moving to San Francisco would be a gay dream."

"Not for me," I countered, trying not to sound as despondent as I suddenly felt.

"You sound as miserable as I do," he said after a few seconds.

"Why are you sad?"

"What am I supposed to do in Foster?" he asked rhetorically. "It's not like it's the dating capital of Texas. I get up, go down to the store, close up, head to the gym, and then come home and watch TV until I fall asleep." He sighed. "Not really the life I dreamt of."

"You know, that doesn't sound so bad to me," I admitted.

"Oh really?" he said with a grin.

I nodded and felt my cheeks get red. "Sounds awesome if it was with you."

His grin turned into a wide smile, and I felt my heart skip a beat. "So how long you gonna be in town?"

My mouth moved faster than my mind. "How long do you want me to be?"

He arched an eyebrow in response.

"I mean, I don't have any plans yet," I lied, knowing I had meant to leave on the first flight after Christmas.

"Hmmm…," he murmured as he pulled me in close. "You want some plans?"

"You offering?" I asked, pressing my face next to his, as happy as I have ever felt.

"I think I am," he said, the joy in his voice clear as a bell.

We got up after a while. He fixed us lunch. We sat across from each other at his dining room table, the smiles on our faces never fading for long. "I'm glad you came home for Christmas," he said between bites of his sandwich.

"I am too," I said, feeling one of his feet stroking one of mine under the table.

"You know, if your house is too crowded, you're always welcome to sleep here," he offered brightly. I noticed he blushed slightly as well, and it was adorable.

"Oh really?" I asked.

"I could sleep on the couch," he clarified.

"If you sleep on the couch, then I'm not interested," I replied suggestively.

He smiled back, and I knew where I was going to be for the rest of my vacation.

"So, your family coming back for Christmas?" I wondered out loud.

He shook his head. "They couldn't make it, and believe it or not, this is one of our busiest times of the year, so I can't leave the store."

"You're going to be here alone?" I exclaimed, shocked.

"It's just a day," he reassured me. "I think I already got what I wanted for Christmas."

It took a while for the smile to fade off my face. And it kept sneaking back every time it faded.

Sometimes a moment in life comes when you have to make a choice you know is going to change everything. You're sitting at a blackjack table staring the Fates in their faces and they are asking you, "Hit or stand?" You can say nothing and let the moment pass, letting the chance go by, leaving your life as it always was. Or you take the hit, daring that is what you need and the results don't destroy your hand. I was miserable, there was no getting around that, and nothing I had done had changed that in the least.

Until now.

"I want you to come to dinner," I blurted.

"What? Where?" he asked back.

"My house," I clarified in a tone that said I thought I had made that point very clear.

"You're serious?" he asked, staring at me like a baby owl.

"I am," I said, putting my sandwich down. "I've never brought anyone before, but I think it's because there isn't anyone I want other than you."

I could see his hesitation; he wasn't out, and though the dinner wasn't going to be telecast on TV, there were going to be a lot of people present. "Why would you want me to go?" he asked after a second.

I stared at the dealer and said, *Hit me.*

"Because I'm tired of being alone, you're tired of being alone," I admitted. "So why not be alone together."

I was worried I had said too much by the way he stared at me with those piercing hazel eyes. Finally he asked, "You've liked me since you saw me reading in the backyard?"

I nodded.

"And if this works out?" he asked.

"I move," I answered instantly.

What the fuck did I just say?

"And if it doesn't work out?"

I smiled. "I never have to come home again."

He laughed at that and nodded. "Okay—fine! I'll come to dinner."

"Can I say you're my date?" I asked, getting up and walking around the table to pull him to his feet and into my arms.

"You can say I'm your date," he said, faking a put-upon sigh. Of course, the grin on his face told the real story. Sighing with a smile.

"And can I squeeze your leg under the table?" I asked, kissing him on the cheek. He pushed me down into the chair next to his, then straddled my hips when he plunked down on my lap facing me.

"Not if you don't want your family to see me take you on the dining room table."

I sat there, staring contemplatively at the ceiling as I pondered.

"What are you doing?" he asked.

"Wondering if sex with you is worth my mother having a heart attack."

He leaned in and kissed me deeply. "Then don't squeeze my leg."

I promised him I would consider it.

While Tyler got dressed, I called my mom and told her I was bringing someone to dinner and to set an extra place.

"You're bringing someone?" she asked in shock.

"I am," I said.

"A man?" she asked.

"He is," I answered.

"A date?" she asked, her voice bursting with joy.

"Is that okay?" I asked.

She half covered the phone and called out. "Johnny! Set another place at the table!"

I had to laugh at that.

We walked down the street toward my house in the dark. Halfway there, he grabbed my hand and nudged me with his shoulder. "This okay with you?" he asked, squeezing my hand just in case I need clarification.

"Is it okay with you?" I countered.

After a second, he nodded. "Normally it wouldn't be. I've lived here so long terrified of people finding out about me that something like this"—he held up our joined hands—"would have caused me to throw up. But for some reason, with you I just don't care."

That made me glow inside.

We got to my house, and I knocked on the door, knowing my mother would want to make a thing of it. She opened the door and looked at me, and then at Tyler, and her smile was infectious. "Oh, it's *you*!" she said, clapping.

I looked over at Tyler and then back. "You know him from down the block?"

She grabbed Tyler's hand and pulled us inside. "No, you silly," she said, closing the door behind us. "I knew I was right!" she crowed.

"What are you taking about?" I asked as we took off our coats.

She turned and looked at us with obvious pride. "This is the boy I was telling you about." I looked even more confused. "*This* is Frances's son!"

I looked over at him with narrowed eyes. "You knew about me?"

He shrugged and smiled. "What can I say?" he said sheepishly. "Um, Merry Christmas?"

TYLER

It was the first time I was another guy's date for dinner.

Matt's brothers kept taking turns looking at me with equal measures of curiosity and hostility. Curiosity because they had no idea I was gay, hostility because they were realizing that a gay guy had owned them on the football field back in high school.

"So, you were gay back then?" the oldest asked me, mouth half full of turkey.

I nodded. "If you'd asked me I would have said no, but yeah, I was."

"But you had a girlfriend," William, the middle one, more pronounced than asked.

"Hey, doofus! Back off," Matt snapped at his brother. I motioned to him that I was okay with the question-and-answer period.

"I did have a girlfriend, who had no idea I was gay because I was in the closet. But I was still gay."

John's eyes narrowed as he stabbed another forkful of meat. "But did you have sex with guys back then?"

Matt's dad slammed his hand on the table. "John! That's enough!"

He ignored his father's admonishment as he waited for an answer from me. I saw that more than a few people were waiting for my answer. I finally admitted, "No, not in high school."

He dropped his fork and cheered as William did the same. They high-fived across the table and went back to the food. I looked over to Matt in confusion. "If you didn't actually have sex then, in their minds, you couldn't have been gay when you beat us." The look on my face must have told him what was going through his mind because he just shook his head. "Hey, I have no idea where they get that from. I'm just telling you what they're cheering about."

"So how are your parents?" Mrs. Wallace asked me. I'm pretty sure she talked to my mom more than I did, so she would know better than I would.

But I smiled and answered, "They're good. I think my dad is bored with Florida, but she loves the sun."

I saw her nod. "She does make Florida sound lovely, but I don't think I could ever leave Foster."

"The winters there have to be better than ours," Mr. Wallace grunted.

John looked up from his plate. "What's wrong with some snow?"

"Plenty, if you're the one who's trying to shovel it or drive through it," his dad complained.

I noticed that Matt and his mom were doing a pretty good job of avoiding eye contact with each other. When William started debating with his father about how much snow was too much, I leaned over to Matt. "What's going on?" He looked at me, a puzzled expression on his face, and I glanced quickly toward his mother and then back at him.

"She's pissed at me," he whispered back.

"What did you do?"

He gave me a shocked look. "Why do you assume I did something wrong?" he whispered.

"Because it's your mom, and that woman couldn't hurt a fly," I whispered back. I had known Mrs. Wallace via my mom for a couple of years and was taken by her incredible kindness. She was also a regular around the shop, though I had to admit I had no idea who she was buying all the gear for. "Whatever you did, go apologize."

He stared into my eyes for a long time and realized I wasn't kidding. "You are really going to make me apologize to my mom? Right now?" When he could see the earnestness in my eyes, he sighed and tossed his napkin on the table. "Mom, you need some help with the pies?"

She looked like she was going to automatically say no but saw him already half standing up and rose to join him.

"Whipped cream?" John asked as they made their way to the kitchen.

Mrs. Wallace turned around. "Eat what's on your plate first before you start demanding more food."

His head went back to his food quickly, as if slapped.

We all sat in silence as we collectively finished our meals.

MATT

I WALKED into the kitchen with the same spring in my steps that I imagine prisoners being led to a firing squad would have.

Mom was pissed, and the way she threw open the oven and yanked out the pumpkin pie more than told me that. I stood there feeling like I was ten years old waiting for a scolding, and it sucked. I went over to try to help her cut the pie, but she ignored me and began to slice it up herself, each motion one of deadly precision. My fingers twitched and insisted on heading for my pants pockets.

I might have underestimated how mad she actually was at me.

"I wanted to say I'm sorry—" I began.

She grabbed a stack of plates from the overhead cabinet and put them beside the pie. "Fine" was all she said.

The coward in me wanted to just say, "Well, I tried," and make a break for the dining room, but I knew better than that. I had screwed up and I needed to make it better. "Mom," I said, moving closer to her. "Can you stop that and look at me?"

She did turn to look at me, and I felt even worse when I saw the hurt and anger in her eyes. "What do you want me to say, Matt? That I'm not mad? That you didn't hurt my feelings—again—by assuming I'm prying into your life? What do you want to hear? Tell me so I can tell you and then get this pie served."

"I didn't say you were prying." Which was about the lamest sentence I could have come up with. We both knew it. Of course I had thought she was prying, but denying it was the only thing that came to mind. She crossed her arms and shot me an angry stare, which told me she wasn't buying it either. "Okay," I amended before she could explode. "I guess I did. But you seem to think I'm always miserable and need help to make me less miserable when I'm not miserable in the first place."

"Yes you are, Matthew," she responded frankly. "You're miserable. You have been since you realized you were gay, and we both know it.

You know, Matt, some parents disown their children when they come out of the closet. Those parents turn their backs on their own flesh and blood because of who they love. If the worst thing you can complain about in your life is that your mother is concerned for your well-being, then you have it a lot better than most. Are we done?"

I felt like my face had been slapped.

"Why does everyone insist on thinking I'm miserable all the time?" I asked, anger creeping into my voice. "Shouldn't I be the one who knows what I am and am not?"

"*That* is the problem," she threw back at me. "You and that horrid woman you pal around with have convinced yourself you aren't, but you are, and it has you stalled. Here you are at an age where you should be thinking about what you're going to do with the rest of your life, and you're still hanging out in bars!"

"And where else am I supposed to meet guys, Mom?" I asked her. Suddenly I didn't care how I sounded. "Do you know a magical place where gay men congregate so I can meet them?"

She didn't back off an inch. "Yes. You can be introduced to them by family and friends, say, over vacation."

I just stood there stunned, not only by how right she was, but by the staggering amount of wrong I had been.

"You are your own worst enemy, Matthew. You always have been," she added with real regret in her voice. "In your entire life, has one person been mean to you about being gay? Ever? I mean, think about it for a second. Have your brothers ever been mean to you because of it? Your dad? Me? Matt, the only person who has a problem with you being gay is you, and I don't know why and I wish I could fix it, but I can't. That's up to you." She turned and picked up the tray with the pie and plates on it. "Come get some dessert."

She stalked out and left me standing there, wondering when exactly my life had broken away from me.

TYLER

THE REST of the night passed with the same sense of awkwardness that can come up during the holidays when all the family gossip has been exchanged and there's still a long time left for conversation that no one seems to be comfortable with.

Matt assured me everything was okay, but it was pretty obvious it wasn't. His family spent the rest of the night talking and catching up while Matt sat in the corner and nursed his eggnog. John let out a huge yawn and announced it was time for him to hit the sack, and the rest of us used it as a signal the night was over.

"I'm going to stay over at Tyler's," Matt told his parents as they cleared the dishes out of the dining room.

His dad raised an eyebrow but said nothing, while his mom tried to pretend she didn't care but hid a smile nonetheless. "Well then, you boys be safe," Mr. Wallace said after a few seconds. Matt got red and his father coughed. "I meant getting home." They both tried to recover from their embarrassment while all of us tried to figure out what to say next.

"It was nice seeing you again, Mr. Wallace," I said, trying to break the tension.

"It's great seeing you too, Tyler," he replied, quickly shaking my hand. "Say hi to your father next time you talk."

"I will, thanks," I assured him as Matt ran upstairs to grab a change of clothes.

Mrs. Wallace reappeared from the kitchen with a covered plate. "I packed you some leftovers," she explained as she handed me the dish. "No one should be without a home-cooked meal around Christmas."

I might have argued with her if her cooking wasn't as good as it was. Instead, I thanked her and took the plate. "Thank you, ma'am, this is very nice of you."

Mr. Wallace looked at her. "Ma'am? Someone raised the boy right."

I chuckled at that. "My dad is big on manners."

71

Just then, Matt clattered downstairs carrying a duffel bag. "I'm ready."

"Thank you again for having me over," I said to them. "It was very nice of you."

"If we were nice, we would have waited until you weren't here to fight," Mrs. Wallace said pleasantly. "You boys have a good time."

"But not *that* good a time," his father added. He glanced at Mrs. Wallace, and they both smiled mischievously. I think they'd waited a long time to be able to say that to Matt, and they were enjoying it.

We, on the other hand, headed for the door before we died of embarrassment.

The night air was crisp, and we walked quickly back to my house. If it had been any farther away than a couple of blocks, the cold would have been damned uncomfortable. I had the advantage of a warm plate full of leftovers to keep my hands from turning into ice cubes. Matt shoved his hands into his jacket pockets and kept up with me, walking silently. I could tell he had a lot on his mind, but he didn't say anything until my house was within sight. "Do you think I'm making a mistake?" he finally asked me.

"In coming over?" I asked him back, confused.

"In the whole thing. I just don't know what I'm doing with my life anymore. Every decision I make usually ends up being the wrong one. Then that decision leads to another decision and another until I'm stuck with a big pile of steaming...."

I had heard rants like this before, usually coming from my own mouth. There were days I felt like I was the worst-case scenario of my life rather than the actual person living it. Like if you had looked at my life and came up with every bad decision a person could make without dying, that would be me. I wasn't a real person; I was a cautionary tale for another me somewhere when the ghosts of Christmas Past showed up. But my meeting Matt felt different. Better. I wanted him to know it too.

So I kissed him.

At first he didn't react. Then, slowly, he began to melt into me, responding to the caress and hopefully forgetting about his unhappiness for one small second. I unlocked my front door and dragged him inside. Still kissing and nuzzling and nipping each other's necks, we kicked the door shut, dropped our jackets, left the plate of food on the little chair in the hall, and headed for my room upstairs. By the time we made it there, we had left a trail of clothes on the steps. I backed in into the bedroom door, still kissing him.

I turned him around and pushed him back onto my bed. For the moment, I smiled and forgot about all my doubts and fears. Pulling off my shirt, I moved toward him, giving way to the desire I'd felt since I saw him in the store.

We stopped just before actual intercourse, not from lack of interest but because we both ended up finishing well before things got that far. Normally that wouldn't have been an issue, but instead of working ourselves into another session of sex, we lay there with each other. He curled himself into my arms and I held him close, just enjoying the feeling of someone sleeping next to me.

And it hit me, right at that moment, at that very second. I was happy. I was truly and completely happy. There was a contentedness in my heart I hadn't felt in… well, ever.

Which was, of course, the very instant I started to panic.

MATT

WELL, THIS is nice.

Yeah, I know, not the best thought to have lying next to the guy you had been in imaginary love with since high school, but there it is. And as incredible as it was that I was lying next to Tyler fucking Parker, the fact remained, I was still upset.

"You okay?" he asked, pulling me closer to him.

I nodded, but it was a lying nod, a nod that had no good intention about it. All that nod could do was lie and ruin people's lives.

Wow, I just imbued a nod with superpowers. I was fucked-up.

"No," I said, sitting up. "I'm just... I mean...."

He was looking at me, waiting for me to finish a coherent sentence.

I had been waiting for that same thing since I was fourteen.

"Look, if this is just sex, then let's say that now."

He cocked his head. "We actually didn't have sex yet."

"You know what I mean."

"I really don't."

"What is this?"

He was quiet for a long while, and I thought he was going to throw me out. There was only so much crazy one guy could take, and I was creeping up on it with a vengeance.

"Okay look, I like you, you like me, so... we like each other."

I nodded.

"And we don't know what that means yet, because we could end up hating each other's guts after three days."

Another nod.

"But we are both looking for something more than sex... right?"

He seemed as unsure as I was.

"I mean...." I trailed off.

What was I going to say? *I'm looking for so much more than sex it would terrify you. I am looking for a well-groomed, athletic prince, horse optional, to come and sweep me off my feet and take me away from all this.* I wanted to go to sleep next to someone knowing they were going to be there in the morning. I wanted to go grocery shopping and figure out what I was going to cook for us. I wanted someone to lie on as I watched TV; I wanted someone to just be there.

I wanted way more than sex.

But what was I going to say? *Actually, I'm shopping around for a happily ever after, I'll take a content for the foreseeable future or even a satisfied for right now, but no, I am not looking to have sex with you and just leave. I want more. I need more. I... I....*

"Yes," I finally said. "I'm looking for more than sex."

He nodded. "And I am too, so this—" He waggled his finger between him and me. "—is more than sex."

This seemed so fucking complicated. "So what if we end up liking each other a lot?"

He smiled. "One of us moves."

My stomach did a backflip, and I told it to fucking chill.

"And if we don't like each other?"

Same smile. "One of us moves."

He made it seem simple, just... just be together. Be happy. Just add water.

I wanted happy; I had some water.

How hard could it be?

"Deal," I said, holding my hand out to shake.

He looked down at it and laughed. "Matt, I just sucked your dick. We don't have to shake on it."

"Right," I said, dropping it quickly.

"We can fuck on it," he added, a mischievous glimmer in his eye.

"Is that how we seal the deal?"

He grabbed me and pulled me in for a kiss. "We do now."

I fell on top of him and stopped worrying. Right now, this felt too good to go wrong.

MATT

"I'll move? Who the fuck says that?" I whined into my cell phone.

Sophia's laugh was half Margaret Hamilton from *The Wizard of Oz* and half Maleficent, voiced by the flawless Eleanor Audley in *Sleeping Beauty*. "Apparently he does, cupcake!" Her cackle was pure evil and chilled me to the bone, even though she was thousands of miles away.

I normally hated her more than the Republican Party, Fox News, and those stretch pants that look like jeans combined, but never more so than when she was right. And once again, she was fucking right.

I had been in lust with the boy who lived down the street since I was old enough to know what lust meant but had never done anything about it as a teen. I had built this entire fantasy around who this boy was and what he would be like if I met him, so much so that it had ended up screwing up any actual relationships I'd tried to have. Now we'd ended up spending Christmas and the next few days after together, acting as if we'd been a couple forever and everything was perfect.

Except the ghost of his words, "I'll move."

"What am I going to do?" I moaned into the phone, hoping my voice didn't carry outside my room and wake my parents. It was already midnight in Foster. People who were awake at midnight in Foster were treading into something akin to no-man's-land as far as the general populace was concerned. Since only bad could come from no-man's-land, being awake and doing strange things like making phone calls was considered a mortal sin, even if your body was still on California time.

"You think Biden has a witness relocation program for hopeless gay people?" she asked, far too much satisfaction in her voice.

"I hate you," I snapped. "Do you think he was joking?" I asked in exactly the tone a blonde bimbo in a B-grade horror flick uses when she calls "Is anyone out there" to a darkened room right after she's had slutty sex with her rebel boyfriend on a dare. It wasn't so much a question as it was a declaration of my own mortality, because I knew the truth was out there in the darkness, just waiting to pounce on me.

"I am sure he's out registering at Bath, Barn and Beyond or whatever hick-ass stores you guys have out there." Sophia's mutant ability allowed her to make even the most insulting of comments without enraging her target. "So have you screwed yet?" she asked. I pictured her leaning forward, one of her Lee Press-On Nails in her teeth as she waited breathlessly for my answer.

"You *do* know someday a fresh-faced teenager is going to throw a bucket of water on you, right?" I replied somewhat weakly after a few seconds.

"That's a yes and it was great," she howled. I felt what was left of my patience dwindle to zero.

"This is serious!" I exclaimed over her hysterics. Her lack of empathy was seriously frustrating me.

Before she could answer, the wall to my right tried to cave in under the force of my father's fist. His muffled but unmistakably angry voice called out, "Matthew! Do you have any idea what time it is?"

Suddenly I was twelve years old again. "Sorry, Dad!" I called out to the wall.

"This is serious!" I hissed into the phone, while images of my dad bursting into the room to tell me that tomorrow was a school day danced in front of my eyes. "What am I going to do?" I stood by my door and listened for my father's footsteps.

"Have you, I don't know, tried *talking* to him about it?"

"Talking is what got me into this trouble in the first place!" I whispered harshly into the phone, my paranoia making phantom sounds come from under my door.

"Honey, you have to talk to him." Sophia's voice lowered into unfamiliar territory, sounding almost sympathetic. "What if he's freaking out as bad as you are?"

I sighed and slid down the door until I sat listlessly on the floor. "No one can be freaking out more than I am right now."

TYLER

"I AM seriously freaking out."

Linda laughed as she signaled the bartender for a couple more beers. "You've been saying that for almost a week now, Tyler," she commented above the music. "Is it that bad?"

I shrugged as Pete slid a cold beer in front of me. "I'm of two minds," I said, taking a long swallow of Shiner Bock.

We walked back to our table, maneuvering between the small clumps of people dancing to the music from the jukebox. "So one mind says?" she asked once we sat back down.

"He's awesome and I love spending time with him," I admitted truthfully.

"Considering this is the first time I've seen you guys apart since you hooked up, I would say that's a no-brainer."

She was right. Matt had spent every night with me since Christmas, and so far, it had been incredible. I felt uncharacteristically domestic, but being domestic had its points.

"But?" she prompted me out of my silence. "The other brain says?"

I tried not to look panicked as I answered. "Who asks someone to move before we even have a date?"

"Maybe he thinks it was a joke?" she offered, though the expression on her face made it clear she didn't believe it either.

"A joke usually has a punch line. This was a statement," I said, taking an even longer drink of my beer. "What if he thought I was serious?"

This time she shrugged. "Were you?"

And there it was, folks, the million-dollar question.

Say it with me: *Did. Tyler. Fuck. Up. Again?*

I put my head on the table as I moaned, "I don't know."

She put a hand on my shoulder in sympathy. "You know, you can't be a slut your entire life." I looked up in shock, and she burst out laughing in response. "I'm kidding!" she added quickly. "Tyler, if you had asked me before Christmas, I would have said you were the one man this side of the Mississippi in most need of a good lay. I think you and Matt are a good thing."

"We just met," I protested, wondering when exactly I ended up sounding so whiny.

"And?" she countered. "You've known each other since we were kids."

That was true and false at the same time, and she knew it.

Matt and his brothers were legendary in their day as kings of high school football around Foster. The Wallace brothers were, as I have put it once, sex in sneakers, and most of my teenage life had been spent fantasizing about one or more of them.

"This is just too fast," I said to the table.

"Can I ask you a question and not get my head bit off?" she asked after a few seconds. I nodded. "You said this before Christmas. Why are you freaking about it now? I mean, has he even brought it up again?"

He hadn't said a word about it, but I knew it was on his mind as well. It was like an elephant that sat between us on the couch as we watched TV. A giant, uncomfortable elephant that refused to go away but neither one of us wanted to talk about.

Linda said nothing as I sat there with my head down, wondering why this was freaking me out so much. When I didn't think, which had been most of this week, everything was great. We had enjoyed exploring ourselves as a couple, which was a completely new thing for me, since the longest relationship I had ever been in was a year and a half, and that had been with a woman. Guys had fallen into the hit-and-run category and lately not even that. When I lived in Florida, I had cruised the web for hookups with other closeted guys and had done pretty well, if I do say so myself.

And then my knee exploded and I moved back to Foster.

I didn't so much hit a dry spell as I realized I had moved into a desert. The closest place that even had a gay bar was a drive away, and after Riley, I was terrified to step foot into it again.

Crap, I hadn't finished explaining that to you, had I?

OKAY, SO for a while things were pretty cool, because I had gay friends for the first time in my life. Riley would call me a couple of days a week and ask if I wanted to head up to the Bear's Den with him and Robbie. Which was an incredible gesture on Riley's part, because he had to know I would have never gone without them. Robbie never said a word to me, but I had the sense he was just barely tolerating me always going with them. However, for Riley's sake, he was staying quiet.

That alone should have won him a Nobel peace prize in my book.

They slowly immersed me in gay culture, coaxing the real me out of the closet step-by-step with equal parts of alcohol, music, and promises of sexual encounters with guys that lasted more than one night, which would be one more night than the ones I'd had before. It was a hard sell, but they kept at it; Riley coaxed me with social carrots, and Robbie wielded a pretty sharp verbal stick when I balked.

"You do know you aren't getting any younger, right?" he'd say to me when I tried to find an excuse for not going. "You're, like, a couple of years away from your body realizing it's midnight, and then, trust me, you're going to wish you'd used what you had when you had it."

I would give him a wry grin. "And what exactly do I have?"

In return I'd get a small pause and a not-small glare and sneer. "Fuck you. I am not feeding that already Godzilla-sized ego you possess. Stay here and get old. *We* are going out."

I'd follow him and Riley out to their car. "No, come on, tell me what I have now! I want to hear you say it."

"I hate this town," he'd tell Riley before slamming the car door behind him.

In the end, I'd end up going with them and liking it.

I spent long hours talking to Riley about the guys we went to school with who we both had a crush on while Robbie listened in and, as a matter of sheer principle, hated every name we brought up. After a month or so, I was invited over to their house for a dinner party of sorts, a chance for me to mingle with other homosexuals in their natural environment, as Robbie put it. I asked them a dozen times if this was just a lame excuse for them to set me up with one of their friends. Each time they denied it, which made me ask again. The asking and denying got so bad that Robbie just threw his arms up at one point and exclaimed, "Fine! Don't come, bitch! I'm sure we can feed another dozen people on what you would eat alone."

I might have said something to defend myself if I hadn't had my mouth full of crackers at the time.

So the night of the party, I forced myself not to panic or to chicken out and showed up at their door with a bottle of decent wine under my arm. Robbie answered the door. His smile was as evil as anything I had seen before and didn't get any nicer when he welcomed me in. "Enter of your own free will, and welcome," he declared, moving aside and taking the wine. "Oh look! Wine without a screw-off cap. See, we *are* having an effect on you." I told him to shove it just as I noticed the startling lack of people in attendance.

"Am I that early?" I asked.

Which was when another guy walked out from the hallway, drying his hands. "Hey, you sure this guy is going to show up?" And then he noticed me and paused. He was a decent-looking guy, but not someone you'd turn your head for. He was a little older than me. No, that was a lie; he was a lot older than me. I'm not saying he was a senior citizen, but this guy was easily ten years older than me if he was a day. He looked me up and down like I was something in a store window instead of a person.

"Okay, it's a lame attempt to set you up with one of our friends. So get over it," Robbie ordered. I noticed he'd taken a position standing in front of the door.

I was about to turn and push him out of the way when Riley came over. That insanely welcoming smile he had caught me squarely between the eyes. "Hey! You made it," he said as warmly as could be. "Have you met my friend Jim? He's the foreman out at my parents' ranch."

I forced myself to smile and shake Jim's hand as if I had been expecting him to be there. "Pleased to meet you," I said robotically.

"Hey there," he said, gripping my hand firmly. "Pleased to meet you."

"Same," I replied, completely on autopilot.

"Great, so we're all here," Robbie added, walking toward the kitchen and staying out of my reach the entire time, I noticed. "How about we pop this baby open and get the night started?" He grabbed a corkscrew and deftly pulled the cork out of my wine bottle with one smooth movement.

"I've heard a lot about you," Jim added as we walked toward the breakfast nook where Robbie was pouring the wine.

"Oh really?" I said, giving Robbie the deadliest glare I had. He ignored it, of course, and smiled innocently as a baby as he handed me a glass of wine.

"Yeah, these two won't shut up about you," Jim explained over a sip of his wine.

"Oh yeah, they can be like that," I said, downing half the glass in one swallow. "Always full of surprises."

"Is there a surprise coming?" Jim asked, confused.

"Count on it," I said, snarling at Robbie before finishing the glass. "Hit me again." I slid the glass back toward him.

"Someone likes cheap wine," he muttered under his breath. Nevertheless, he filled my glass again.

"So, Tyler runs the sporting goods store over on First Street," Riley said in an attempt to break the tension.

"Oh? Is that fun?" Jim asked, doing a good job at faking interest. Well, except for the word "fun," which he hadn't meant to say, I think. His face pinked up a little when he realized how he sounded.

"It pays the bills," I said, desperately trying to find a way to get out of this without being a complete asshole.

There were a few seconds of uncomfortable silence before Jim offered, "I handle the steers over on the ranch."

"Oh, is that fun?" I asked him, looking for an escape hatch nearby.

"It pays the bills."

It took me a couple of seconds to process he had given me my own answer back. I tried to laugh, but it sounded so mangled I just stopped. "I'm sorry. Robbie, can I talk to you for a moment?" He paused in the kitchen and pointed at himself questioningly. "Yes, you," I growled, striding down the hall to get away from the living room.

We ducked back into one of the spare rooms. "What in the hell is this?" I demanded.

"Oh no, ma'am," he countered, taking a step back from me. "Do not come at me like I owe you money or something. You want to have a conversation? That's fine, but you best check yourself before you wreck yourself."

His attitude made me want to scream even louder, but I took a deep breath and tried again. "What exactly do you think you're doing out there?"

He arched one eyebrow. "Well, I was making sure the chicken didn't get burnt, but I have a feeling you aren't talking about my culinary skills." I was about to start yelling again, but he held up a finger and paused me. "What I think I am doing is trying to get you to meet another living, breathing gay man who you can date. You know, in some cultures that might be looked on as a good thing, but leave it to Foster to fuck up even a blind date."

"I didn't ask you to set me up."

He shrugged. "No one asks to be set up. Well, I guess some do, but those are just pathetic losers who aren't going to get laid anyway, so they don't count." I was about to go off again, but he just kept talking. "Yes, we tried to set you up, and yes, we lied to you because you are basically a twelve-year-old girl when it comes to anything resembling relationships, and if we told you anything, you would have just ran screaming into the night."

I opened my mouth, but he just kept going. "And yes, I know it isn't cool to just jump out with a guy you don't know, but that is the price you pay for being emotionally stunted when it comes to the whole dating thing. No one is expecting you and Jim to get married! Hell, I thought he was too old for you, but Riley thought it would be easier to start you out with a pony before you tried to ride a real horse, and no, that isn't a dick joke."

I tried again to talk but he ignored me. "It might as well be, since all you know are one-night stands. So just go out there and pretend to like him for tonight, and then we can regroup and grade you on how well you did."

I opened my mouth again to respond and then closed it again as I realized I had forgotten what I was going to say.

"Good," Robbie said, grabbing my arm and turning me around. "So let's head out and learn to play nice with others, okay?"

I let him lead me back to the living room in a daze as I wondered when exactly I had lost control of the night.

"SO THEN dump him," Linda said once she realized I had stopped talking.

I looked up at her and shook the past out of my head. "I hope you don't give Kyle that kind of advice!" I exclaimed.

She waved her finger at me. "No, do *not* bring my son and his boyfriend into it. So far, they know more about gay dating than you seem to, so keep them out of it. If you are that bent out of shape, tell him it's moving too fast and break up with him."

"I don't want to," I answered, sounding like I had regressed to the age of six and two-thirds.

"Then there's your answer, isn't it?" She smiled back at me.

"But I'm freaking out!" I screamed as the music stopped. Everyone in the bar looked over at us, and I felt my face turning six shades of red.

"Drama queen," she called to them, grinning. "What can I do?"

"You suck," I said as everyone laughed and the music started back up.

"And you are a chickenshit," she fired back. "If you like Matt, then like him. He knows you were joking, and you know it, you're just creating an excuse to run." She finished her beer and slammed the bottle down on the table hard, the only indication of how much she'd drunk. "Now, I promised Kyle that I was going to try to fly straight, so I'm calling a cab and going home."

I felt myself sober up some. "What is going on with them?"

She shrugged as she pulled out her cell. "Kyle's been obsessed with some guy named Kelly. He won't tell me what's up, but knowing

Kyle, he's trying to do something good for someone else. I try to stay out of his way when he's that set on something."

"You are a very cool mom," I informed her, smiling.

She didn't smile back. "No, I'm not. Kyle has lived through some shit because of me, and that's on my soul. But damned if I'll let other people treat him like shit for something like being gay. I saw how it killed you when we were his age. It's not going to happen, not again."

She gave the cab dispatcher her address as I finished my beer.

I had a hard time seeing Linda as a mom. She had always been such a party girl growing up. I had no idea what she'd meant about Kyle, but I had a feeling his being hassled at school might have been the wake-up call she needed.

"You okay?" she asked before hanging up.

I nodded as I pulled on my jacket. "Yeah, the walk home'll sober me up some. 'Sides, not a lot of street crime in Foster." I tossed a few bills down for a tip. "Tell Kyle hi and stuff for me?" I said as I turned to walk out.

I heard her voice rise to a pretty good impression of a gay lisp as she recited, "'Kyle, I saw your aunt Tyler last night, and she said, between having a panic attack because a boy likes her, hi and stuff.'"

My answer was a lone finger as I walked out into the bracing cold of the December air. I hunkered down into my jacket as I began the long walk. I had no freaking idea what macho bullshit had convinced me I didn't need a ride home. The second gust of wind tore through me, chilling me as if I were naked. Bullshit or not, there I was nonetheless, and home I'd better get. Quick.

"It's tough being a stubborn queer," I said to myself as my teeth began to chatter from the cold. My feet wandered toward my neighborhood while I pondered how much of my "success" in sports had been because I had been determined not to come off gay in any way, shape, or form to even the sharpest eyes. Not that I had believed I was obvious from the outside or anything, but I had been terrified back then that someone would be able to clock me from the way I looked at a guy too long or licked my lips unconsciously. My fears seemed silly now, but when I was just a pup, keeping my shit secret was my entire life.

Most of the time I like to think I've grown as a person, but then I find myself walking home when it's colder than a witch's tit because my ego thinks it's what a straight guy would do.

I had walked five blocks so far and hadn't seen a soul, straight or otherwise.

My thoughts began to drift, which was the problem with thinking about Riley and Robbie when drunk. Once the Pandora's box that was my brain opened, there was no getting that crap back inside until I finished the entire story. I wished I could. I wished I could just go in and erase the last part of the story and end it there at the memory of being set up for an incredibly bad blind date by two friends who were only trying to make me happy. That'd be a nice story, right? There were these two boys and they fell in love. Who couldn't enjoy that?

My "agreement" to that first blind date implied a silent consent to others, as far as Riley and Robbie were concerned. My consent resulted in about two months of sporadic dates with gay single guys Robbie and Riley knew. The whole dating thing was surprising in a couple of ways. One, I had to acknowledge I might have been more than a little picky when it came to dating. Some of the dates were with guys I'd met since I'd been going to the Bear's Den, but who hadn't set anything off in my mind interest-wise. Robbie told me I could afford to be picky as long as I kept myself in shape. He also informed me that personalities wear pen protectors sometimes. Two, there were far more gay people around Foster than I would ever have guessed. Most of them weren't from Foster proper but worked around the area in oil or on one of the ranches. How the dynamic duo found them, I never asked; I just agreed to meet the boy du jour and be as nice as I could manage. The third surprising thing was how they never gave up on finding me a man.

I don't know if it was pity or if they were trying to earn some weird gay Boy Scout badge, but the two of them were determined to find me some romance; they wanted to see me happy more than I did. I had long ago given up the ghost as far as finding someone in Foster and had just moved on, or so I liked to think. But not these guys. Before Riley and Robbie, I would have found that kind of intrusion into my carefully hidden personal life offensive and annoying. However, for some reason,

I felt neither. It was nice to have gay friends; it was something new for me, and I planned on enjoying it.

So it made what happened next that much more god-awful.

We had all agreed to meet at the Bear's Den one Friday night to see if we couldn't figure out a better way of finding me a guy, since the local population was not getting the job done. Even though I was known at the Den, I still waited in my car for them to show up so I could walk in with them. I have no idea why I still did it—most likely a defense mechanism in case someone saw me out there. I could say I was friends with Riley and was being an open-minded friend instead of a fellow gay man.

And yes, that excuse sounded just as lame to myself then as it does to you now.

I saw Robbie shake his head at me when I got out of the car once they showed up. Riley never said anything about me staying outside and acted as if he didn't notice, but not Robbie. "Oh look, it's Foster's very own Goldilocks. Oh no! That boy is too old, that boy is too gay, oh, when will I ever find one who's just right?" Robbie had a hand on his forehead as he struck a damsel-in-distress pose.

"You do know I can kick your ass, like, fifteen different ways, right?" I said, grinning.

"Oh, bitch, *please*. You think you're so tough. Try surviving clearance day at Valentina's when she marks down the good wigs. You got nothing on New York drag queens." He snapped his fingers twice at me, and I felt sufficiently shut down.

"I tell you not to get into it with him, and what do you do?" Riley asked as he opened the door for me.

"He ain't so tough," I said under my breath.

"Yeah, I notice you said *that* just quiet enough so he couldn't hear," he teased me as we walked in.

I wish I could tell you there was something different about that night from all the other ones, but I can't. That there was something we talked about or something that happened to make that Friday night unique and stand out in my mind, but I'd be lying. The only thing that made that night different was that it was the last one.

We hung out until after last call, when Tom would turn on the bar lights and most guys would scurry away like cockroaches caught in the kitchen in the middle of the night. It wasn't the first time Robbie, Riley, and I had closed the place down. It was business as usual. We helped Tom pick up around the tables as we tried to sober up enough to drive. "The boy with the blue shirt was cute," Robbie suggested as I grabbed a couple of empty beer bottles off a table.

"If he's so cute, you date him," I threw back.

"Hey," Riley protested. "He wasn't cuter than me, right?"

Robbie moved over and kissed him on the cheek. "No one is cuter than you, sweetheart." Riley nodded and went back to cleaning. Robbie turned on me. "And there was nothing wrong with him, and you know it."

"I honestly didn't even notice him," I lied, knowing if I brought up that the guy in the blue shirt was nowhere near my type, it would start another debate about me lowering my standards, and I wasn't ready for that conversation again. "Next time, point him out."

He shot me a dirty look, but there was no way he could prove I had seen Blue Shirt Guy, so he dropped it. "What else you want us to get, Tom?" he asked, dumping another load of empties into the trash.

"How about out of here?" Tom suggested. "I can pick all this up tomorrow, you know."

"My mom always taught me to pick up after myself. Besides, I've worked enough bars to know that this is too much for one guy."

"Riley, you want to control your man?" Tom complained.

"Well, there is no evidence up to this point that anyone can, but I can try," he said, ducking under Robbie's retribution roundhouse swing. Riley lunged toward Robbie, hoisted him up off the ground, and slung him over his shoulder. "Will this work?" he asked, his face lit up with a huge smile.

Tom pointed at the door. "Begone! And never darken my door again."

"Riley, put me down!" Robbie shrieked, pounding on his lover's back.

"Okay, I am out," I said, putting on my jacket. "Riley, are we watching the game this weekend?"

He paused, Robbie still dangling over his shoulder. "Who's playing?"

"It's A&M against Arkansas and Texas at Baylor," I answered, standing in the doorway.

"You can come over if you want. This one won't be up till after noon," he said, bouncing Robbie once.

"Sounds good. I'll bring a case of Shiner," I said, waving as I walked out into the cold.

I wish I'd known that would be the last time I'd talk to him, because I would have picked a different topic than college football and beer. I got into my car and started it up so the heater would kick in. I sat in my car and shivered as I watched the bar door open and Robbie run out ahead of Riley. He had a pretty good head start on his husband, and I smiled as I saw the joy in their eyes as they ran.

With the headlights off, I didn't even see the other car until it was right on top of Riley.

It hit him at midwaist, and time stopped as I watched his body fold in a way I had only seen in tackling dummies. He rolled half onto the hood and then off over the driver's side. His arms just dangled as he fell to the asphalt, and I knew it was bad. A window rolled down from the car, and I saw a head stick out and yell something back at Riley's motionless body.

In less than a second, the car was gone into the night.

Now here is the part of the story I dread the most. You'd think that would be watching my friend get run down in the middle of the road, but you'd be wrong. A normal human being would take Riley's senseless death as the low point of the night, but leave it to Tyler Parker to take it to a whole new level of bad. I saw Robbie run back toward him and shake him slightly. I could hear him cry over the noise of the car and the heater, and it was like nails on a chalkboard. I just sat there and watched him.

Tom came out and stood at the doorway for a moment, trying to see what the commotion was. Once he saw Riley not moving, he rushed back inside to call the cops, which was when my mind began to panic. I couldn't be here. I couldn't talk to the police about this. Suddenly my excuse that Riley was my gay friend and that I was just being nice coming out there sounded like the bullshit it was, and I freaked. There would be witness statements and a police investigation, and that meant an article in the paper.

And my mind screamed at me to get the fuck out of there.

I shifted and began to pull out of the driveway, making sure to avoid the scene entirely. As I was pulling away, Robbie looked up at me, and we made eye contact for just a second. Less than a second, if I'm being honest, but it was all the time in the world. More than enough time for him to scream my name to help him as I drove away. More than enough time for me to look away and take off into the night toward town, in much the same way the guilty party did after killing my friend. Less than a second, but more than enough time for a friendship to end, for me to betray Robbie's trust, and to leave him all alone with his dead lover in his arms.

I want to tell you that I drove away because I thought Riley would be okay. I want to lie to you and myself that I didn't think it was that bad and I just misjudged the seriousness of it, but I can't. Here in the middle of the night, wandering the streets of Foster drunk off my ass, it's only me, you, and the demons that come to me when I close my eyes and think of Riley, and I find it impossible to lie.

I knew he was dead the second he hit the ground, and I still drove away.

Keeping my secret, maintaining my perceived heterosexuality, was so important to me that I left them there and drove away, glancing up at the rearview mirror and seeing them getting smaller and smaller. I've hated myself ever since. Robbie never tried to talk to me, and I never expected him to. I didn't go to the funeral because I didn't want to explain why I was there to others, but more because I knew Robbie would most likely kill me where I stood.

So my life became a series of ever more strangling and entangling lies to protect myself. To escape the truth, I drank myself into a stupor that ended up almost killing me.

The first time I saw Brad and Kyle at Nancy's and saw that they were so obviously in love, something snapped inside me. When I saw Brad, soaking wet and miserable, stumble out of the Vine, I knew I could just turn around and walk back into the shop. I could have just ignored him and what I saw and let him run into the same idiotic walls I spent my life creating so I could slam my head against them. I could; it would have been easy.

But I was done with easy. I was done with hiding. So I stopped Brad outside the shop and turned another corner in my life.

At least, I thought I was through with hiding before Matt. Was I making the same old mistakes over again with him? Was settling down with him one of those gay things I had been running from my whole life? I'd have to give up any illusion that I might be mistaken for straight if I ended up playing house with him. Was that even important to me anymore? I mean, the fact I was even asking the question meant the illusion of being straight had to still matter, right?

Fuck! I was more confused than I had been in the bar. The walk home was supposed to sober me up, not muddle my thinking even more. But the more I thought about it, the more I was convinced I was being colossally stupid. I'd said one of us moves as a joke, but as with all humor, the joke held a grain of truth.

I looked up and was not shocked to see where my feet had led me while I was occupied with my thoughts.

I was standing in front of Matt's house.

The Wallace house had always been much larger than ours. Even when my dad added the back porch with its infamous red door, our home was still barely half the size of Matt's. Of course, I was an only child and the Wallace brothers were, in high school, built like a team of Clydesdales. It sounds like an exaggeration, but if I had seen them pulling a Budweiser truck down the street back then, I wouldn't have thought twice about it. By default, then, their house had to be huge enough to hold them and their belongings. In my drunken estimation, the Wallace house still looked like a boy's house. I could see two Frisbees on the roof, no doubt left up there for years, survivors of a game called when no one wanted to climb up and snag them. A huge tree grew in the front yard, its branches dipping close to the upstairs windows, pretty much guaranteeing it had been used at least once to sneak out after midnight.

I was pretty sure which window was Matt's, and I suddenly had a burning desire to talk to him face-to-face—to let him know I was being an asshole and I understood what he had said was just a joke. I wanted to say out loud that I was in for the long haul, that I wanted to try something serious with him. Talking to him wouldn't wait until the morning; it couldn't. I was ready to be openly gay, and I needed to tell him now.

Before I lost my nerve again.

I'd seen this before in movies. You pick up a pebble and toss it at their window. Do it enough times and they wake up, open it to look down, flash them a smile.

Boom, instant love.

I knelt down and felt the edge of their lawn for a rock or an acorn, something I could toss at his window to wake him up. I had to catch myself from falling face-first into the grass twice before I found a quarter-size rock with the tips of my fingers. I threw it at his window and heard it ricochet off the side of their house. I cursed under my breath as I knelt down, looking for another. I found a smaller one and threw again. I didn't hear anything this time, and I figured I'd missed the house completely. I was mumbling a few choice words under my breath while I searched for something else to throw. I looked for more than a minute before my fingers touched a stone. It was the largest one yet, and I was not going to waste it. I took a few steps closer to his window and wound up for the pitch—

The sound of breaking glass echoed throughout the neighborhood.

Years wasted with friends who thought breaking stuff defined a really fun time had trained me to not stop and gawk at the broken window and the muffled screams coming from the house. Instead my traitorous feet, responsible for bringing me to Matt's in the first place, spun me toward my house and hurtled me down the street, panicked because I had just chucked a boulder through my potential boyfriend's window at two thirty in the morning.

By the time that fact sank in, I was almost home.

I remember a time I could have made that sprint and not been out of breath. I stood with my hands on my thighs in front of my house, my face wreathed in clouds of breath like the smoke coming off a steam engine, the air was so cold. Lights blinked on in houses all over the neighborhood, the commotion from the Wallace house waking other people up like a chain reaction. I fumbled for my keys, praying I hadn't dropped them during my rock search.

God obviously favored innocents, which I wasn't, and idiots, which included drunk people like me. I felt the cold metal in my hand as the lights across the street came on.

I was halfway into my house when I heard a voice call from across the street. "Tyler?"

I paused and turned around, standing in the doorway for a moment, my heartbeat sounding like a shotgun in my own ears. "Hey, Ms. Costello," I called out to her. I looked down the street toward Matt's house, feeling like I was in a very bad melodrama where I was playing guilty neighbor number three.

"What's going on out there?" she asked, looking down the street too.

"No idea," I said carefully. "Maybe kids?"

She sighed heavily and shook her head. "They never learn," she said, retreating into her house.

"Have a good night!" I called out to her, feeling like I had just gotten away with murder. She didn't answer as she slammed her door.

I closed mine and locked it behind me as I took a deep breath. I decided I'd just call Matt when I was sober.

MATT

I SPENT most of the night cleaning up broken glass and trying to assure my mom we were not the victims of a hate crime.

Some kids threw a rock through the window of what used to be my brother's old room close to 3:00 a.m. and all hell broke loose. My mom started screaming while my dad came charging out of his room with a shotgun, in his slippers.

And nothing else.

Recovering from the shock of learning that my dad either slept nude or had gotten lucky that night, I was barely able to keep him from storming out of the house like Clint Eastwood in *Gran Torino*. Only the threat that the people across the street loved to video everything slowed him down. He revved back up again, and I asked him if he wanted to be on an episode of *Grandpas Gone Wild*. Snarling threats, he retreated to the bedroom to put on some clothes.

My mother would only come out of her room after I assured her that, one, there were not armed people in the house, and two, I was going to clean up the broken glass myself.

Nothing dispels Mom-fears faster than the threat of one of their sons cutting themselves on broken glass.

She took the broom away from me and began systematically cleaning the glass up faster than I could have ever done. Once my dad put the shotgun away and put on pants, we got a board from the garage and put it up over the hole. By that time, there was no way any of us were going back to sleep. So my dad made some coffee while my mom made us breakfast. They hovered around the TV, thinking the local news would surely lead with the "Wallace house gets window broken" story and were mildly disappointed when the anchor said nothing.

Around seven thirty, my dad looked at me and said very seriously, "Do not blame what happened on yourself, son."

Which was, to date, the strangest thing ever said to me. I had been blaming the rock, so Dad's pronouncement caught me off guard.

"Say what?" I asked after a few seconds of stunned silence.

"If those people have a problem with your life and feel the need to break our windows, that is *not* your fault." He said it so grimly that I almost burst out laughing. I stopped myself before a giggle could escape my mouth. Dad was serious, and so was Mom. The hair on the back of my neck rose a little as I thought through what had really happened, at least as Dad and Mom saw it.

"Um, okay, Dad. Thank you for being there. I won't blame myself." The energy it would take to convince my dad that the broken window was just stupid kids and not a protest against my sexuality was too much for me to scrape together after being jolted awake at the ass-side of the night. I got up and put my plate in the sink. "I'm going to go take a run and see if Mr. Jensen is at Nancy's having breakfast. If he is, maybe I can convince him to open the hardware store early."

"You think it's safe to run on the street?" my mom asked.

I bit back the automatic sarcasm a question like that normally generated in my mind and instead gave her the most serious look I could muster. "If we change the way we live, Mom, the terrorists win."

She rolled her eyes at me as my dad chuckled a bit. "Okay, smartass, go jog."

I walked over and hugged my mom tightly. "It was just some kids, Mom. I'm fine." She nodded and hugged me back, but I could tell she was still worried. "You do know that John, Billy, and I did much worse than just break a window when we were kids, right?"

She batted at me as she turned back to the stove. "Don't tell me that. Let me keep the illusion my three boys were all angels."

"Yeah, angels with halos propped up on their horns," my dad mumbled from behind his paper.

That made her smile, and I felt marginally better. As I changed in my room, it started to dawn on me how much they must have worried about me being gay if their reaction to a broken window was to automatically blame homophobes. Tyler had told me more about the whole blow-up at Foster High when the baseball player had come out and the drama it had raised before the Christmas break. As I slipped on some sweats, I began to realize how earth-shattering even dealing with an openly gay student, much less an athlete, must be for this town.

In my time, heads would have exploded. Literally exploded all *Scanners*-style with blood and brains everywhere.

The morning sun hung lazily in the distance, and the cold air made me gasp in shock. I rationally knew once I began running I would warm up, but it was hard to resist the urge to turn back and dive under my covers. Then the memory of Tyler's perfectly sculpted abs came to mind, and I could feel my mom's Christmas dinner expanding my waist to the size of a Hula-Hoop.

It's amazing how motivating dating someone better-looking than you are can be when it comes to working out.

I remember loathing this run when I was a teenager. My brothers and I had always been out on the pavement by the time the sun crested the horizon, each of us motivated by different desires. As the oldest, John felt it was his place to set the pace by being our unofficial trainer, making sure we were up and dressed whether we wanted to run or not. Billy, as the next oldest, felt it was his job to keep up with John. I ran because I thought I could make myself more normal by sheer force of will. It was the same reason I had gone into sports, dated girls, and even went through a chewing-tobacco phase one summer. My brothers were more than just my siblings; they were my heterosexual camouflage, the people I hid behind even while my growing feelings were threatening to drive me crazy as a teenager. I assumed that if I looked like them, talked like them, and walked like them, then people would assume I was just like them. So if they were up at 0'dark thirty to run, so was I.

I ran because I didn't want people to notice how many times I walked by the Parkers' house. I ran hoping it would deflect how my eyes lingered in the locker room even though I knew if I was caught, it would mean a fate worse than death. Back then, I was running away from myself and everything I knew I was turning into.

Now I ran because I wanted to keep myself attractive to the very boy I had stalked.

There is no way I could convince you there wasn't a supersized amount of pride in my head that I had actually ended up with the object of my teenage desire. I'm not that good a liar. But that pride was tempered with the growing dread that things were already fucked-up. As I came up Elm toward First Street, all the anxieties I had complained to Sophia about last night came back tenfold.

We weren't fifteen anymore, and just coming out and saying you wanted to be with someone was the gay equivalent of being a Tourette's sufferer with a megaphone. Gay men didn't say that out loud, not to me, at least. Sure, there were the few who seemed to just fall into relationships and didn't mind, but I was never one of those guys. I was always going out with guys who seemed to think dating was like gay chicken—the first one to admit it lost. And my little "I'll just move" was the worst equivalent of dropping an atomic bomb on us. There was no way this was going to work out, I was wasting my time, Tyler would realize he was just joking and this wasn't more than sex, and I would be even sadder than I was because I would have convinced myself it was real.

Right here, right now, I still had the peace of mind to know it wasn't real.

Right?

Nope, not going there. This is a mistake.

The best I could do at this point was quietly back away from Tyler and hope we could salvage a friendship out of this. By the time I passed Foster High, I had decided I would make up some excuse about work and say I had to leave early. If he wanted to call me again, he could call; if he didn't, then that was okay too.

Well, it wasn't okay, but it was better than him telling me he had made a mistake.

I finished the lap around the school and made my way back home— no, I mentally corrected myself, I made my way back to my parents' house. Then I could go home.

Wherever that might be.

TYLER

WHILE I slept, a small family of raccoons had burrowed into my brain and made themselves what was, no doubt from all the extra room between my ears, a spacious home for themselves and their children. That was the only explanation for the roaring headache. I stayed completely still under the covers, afraid to move and make the pain worse. I'd had hangovers before, true. Comparing those hangovers to the crushing weight on my temples and nausea in my stomach was like comparing a splinter in your finger to losing an arm. Most of the time, if I lay real still, the agony would be minimized, but from the moment I opened my eyes, there was nothing I could or could not do to escape the torment. No, there was no way to escape this short of killing myself.

When I was in college, I remember drinking all night, catching a two-hour nap before heading out to my first class, and still having enough energy to make practice that afternoon. As I stood under the hot water splashing from the showerhead, I wondered where exactly that boy with the steel constitution had gone.

With all the speed of frozen sap, I changed and felt my way down to the kitchen, where I hoped an IV of caffeine might be handy. As a backup, if the caffeine didn't work, maybe those electrical paddles EMTs use to bring people back to life; either way, I needed help to wake up. As I silently prayed to my coffee maker to heal me, I shaded my eyes from the rays of the morning sun. What sun worshippers thought of as a warm, light embrace seemed to me to be harsh beams intent on melting my brain with their laser-like intensity. Though I couldn't prove it, I swore I could see the bones of my hand exposed like an x-ray, the light was so bright.

"Fuck this," I said to myself way too loudly. Wincing and annoyed, I stormed off into the living room.

Forty-six seconds later and hidden behind the extra-dark polarizing lenses of my sunglasses, I stalked back into the kitchen. The darkness helped dampen the pain in my head from intolerable to just this side of agonizing. I poured myself a cup of liquid salvation and prayed to the gods of caffeine to save me from this hell of my own making. There were mornings I would have drunk straight from the coffeepot if it wouldn't have scalded me.

I don't know if it was the caffeine or the daily ritual, but as I sat there working on my third cup, the pounding faded slightly and the feeling I was going to vomit everything I had eaten since 2003 went away. I turned on the news as I ate a banana, trying to piece together exactly what had happened last night. I remembered drinking with Linda, worrying about Matt, and then….

And then there was a knock on my door.

Slowly I moved toward the sound of jackhammers on the other side of my front door, completely ready to strangle whoever was making so much noise.

The sun that came blasting as I opened the door blinded me for a moment, and all I could see was the dark outline of a person. Even from that, I could tell it was Matt. "Oh jeez, come in quickly," I urged as I tried to hide behind the door.

He entered at what could only be considered a leisurely pace. "I had no idea I was dating Joan Crawford," he commented on my sunglasses as soon as I closed the door.

"Really?" I asked. "I don't get hot vampire? The first place you go to is Joan fucking Crawford?"

"Vampires don't clutch their coffee mugs with such zeal unless they have blood in them." He leaned over and looked in my cup. "Nope, no blood."

"Morning," I grumbled, stalking back to the kitchen for a refill.

"Good morning to you too," he replied, way too chipper for the hour.

"Did I say it was a good morning?" I asked as I filled my mug again and poured one for him. "I was stating a fact. It is morning. And unless I died last night and this is just some kind of coma-induced hallucination, there is nothing good about it." I handed him his coffee and saw him staring at me intently, as if waiting for me to say something else. "Except you being here, of course. That is a very good thing," I added quickly, leaning in for a kiss.

He kissed me back, but it was a far cry from our usual kisses. Normally, once our mouths got that close to each other, it was a good five to ten minutes before we could pull them apart, and usually that was just to get to a more comfortable place to continue. He walked over and pulled some milk out of the fridge. Trying to focus through the fog in my head, I wondered what had changed.

"Everything okay?" I asked as he started adding sugar to his cup.

"Just a long night." He sighed, not looking at me. "Some kids threw a rock and broke a window, which of course woke my parents up and it was drama and my dad thinks it was a hate crime and it was just stupid and I am going back to San Francisco," he finished, looking at me.

I had caught every other word he had said, and even then it didn't make much sense. The only thing that registered was he was leaving. "Wait. What?" I asked after a few seconds.

He leaned against the counter and sipped at his drink. "I need to get back to work," he said, still not making eye contact, which was Matt for "I am not telling the entire story."

"I thought you took some time off," I replied, which came out a whole lot more aggressive than I meant it to.

"I did," he answered in a clipped tone. "And now I'm going back."

If I thought I felt bad from the hangover, that was nothing compared to the way Matt's words made me feel. My eyes stung as if I had been struck on the nose, and there was an ache in my chest, I mean an honest-to-God pain in my chest where my heart was. Several hundred retorts flashed in my mind. A few dozen "Please don't go" followed by "But I was just getting used to this" a couple of different ways. That impulse was followed by a deep hurt which begged me to ask "What did I do wrong?" and then settled on an arrogant "I didn't do anything wrong" which shifted into an angry "Well then, go." All of this was compressed in my brain and filtered through my common sense and came out my mouth as a surprised,

"Oh. Well... okay." I had no idea what else to say, and the silence was moving from awkward to downright violent.

His eyes locked with mine, and we stayed silent for what felt like a long-ass time.

"Okay," he echoed, his voice sounding like it was coming from somewhere else. Like there was another Matt behind him somewhere doing a pretty crappy ventriloquist act. "Well, just wanted to let you know."

"Thanks," I said, not trusting myself to say anything more because I was moving from shocked to pretty fucking pissed faster than I was comfortable with.

When it was obvious I wasn't going to say anything else, he put the coffee mug down. "Great." He looked around the kitchen for a few seconds like he was searching for something and then back to me. "Okay, then. Well... I'll see you around, Tyler."

And then he swung his fist at me, hitting me squarely in the gut, taking my breath away. Completely shocked, I fell to my knees as his knee came up and connected with my chin. My head flew back as I was thrown onto the tile floor, and my vision blurred as he glared down at me. I tried to say something, but he started kicking me in the side as hard as he could. All I saw were flashes of red when I closed my eyes and tried to block them.

Actually, he held out his hand as if to shake mine goodbye, but the punching and kicking were what I felt.

I shook it numbly. "Have a nice flight, Matt" was all I could mumble.

He might have said something after that, but I honestly couldn't tell you. It took me a few seconds to realize I was alone in the kitchen and he had walked out. Suddenly the hangover was the farthest thing from my mind. I roared angrily and threw the coffee mug against the far wall.

Then I sank to the floor and cried for a while... you know what? No offense, but I don't feel like talking anymore. Can you come back later?

MATT

DON'T TALK to me right now.

There will be a brief intermission while we find someone to narrate the story from here.

Linda Stilleno

When I woke up, it was almost noon.

From the silence that came from the other side of my bedroom door, it was obvious Kyle was already up and gone, which meant I had let him down again. I two-thirds fell, one-third rolled out of bed and grabbed my pack of cigarettes and lighter when my fingers accidentally touched them. Mostly vertical, I squinted until I could spot the bedroom door. I stumbled over my shoes but never dropped the cigarette or the lighter, even managed to light the cigarette without burning my fingers to a crisp. Still fogged mentally, I staggered through last night's crime scene. Because that was what the living room was as far as I was concerned.

I had been so good, coming home early—well, early for me, at least—and had been dead set on seeing my son and spending some time with him during actual daylight hours at least *one* time before the end of his senior year in high school.

That was the plan until Brandon and his friends came by after the bars had closed. And then the plan went to shit.

The smoke almost immediately calmed me down, but I was pretty sure it had nothing to do with the nicotine and more to do with the routine. I had smoked since before I was Kyle's age, and by this time it was the ritual—shaking the cigarette out, tamping the end down on the package, clamping my lips around the filter and lighting up, the sound of the butane igniting as clear as a bell, then the snap of the top of the lighter accompanied by my first deep drag—rather than the actual drug that calmed me down. Brandon had brought a bottle of something, and his friend, Dan I think, had some weed, which only made everything worse. I vaguely remembered we might have done something stronger than weed, but I couldn't remember what. I know we had talked before I ushered them out the door just as the morning news signaled the start of the day.

I needed a shower and some food before I was even close to being able to face how bad I had screwed up last night. Kyle had taped a note on my door telling me he was with Brad and would be back later. That was Kyle's way of telling me he was hurt about my behavior but not the least bit surprised.

I was on my way to the shower when the phone rang. As always, I prayed nothing had happened to Kyle.

"Hello?" I answered, trying to sound as awake as possible. My eyes complained when I forced them wide open, but at least I felt more alert.

"He's leaving," Tyler choked from the other end of the phone.

Without hesitation, I said, "Come over."

Thirty minutes and a shower later, I opened the front door in response to a faint knock. The saddest man in Foster, Texas, stood there.

I'd known Tyler since junior high, and there had never been a time I didn't love him like a brother. There had been something slightly off about him, something I was too young to identify when we first starting hanging out, but something that kept me from lusting after him since I first understood what boys were for. Always the cutest boy in our group of friends, Tyler was the bronze ring of the carousel ride that was high school. Trust me when I say more than a few girls were chasing him in big, bad way.

To me he was always just too sad for words.

Someone glancing at him for a few seconds might easily have missed the clues, but the sadness lay there, visible in his eyes. To me, Tyler always seemed to be on the verge of tears. I opted to be his friend since there was no chance in hell I was going to wade through all that crazy just to jump his bones.

We were out cruising First Street in his father's old Chevy when what made Tyler different—and so sad—finally clicked.

The Wallace brothers were walking out of the Vine Theater. Let me assure you, when the Wallace brothers walked out of, into, along, or across *anywhere*, people stopped and watched. Years later, all I can remember when I think of them is faded 501s, beat-to-hell sneakers, and a trio of lettermen jackets that looked as if they had been tailor-made to show off their small waists and wide shoulders. Damned if I could describe their individual faces, but I didn't really need to. There was something so male about them that to me and most of the girls I was friends with back in the day, the Wallace brothers were the closest thing we had to porn.

That afternoon, when I pulled my gaze away from them, I noticed Tyler was still watching them walk away. The sadness on his face had gone to war with another emotion I couldn't figure out at first. Want, longing—suddenly, Tyler made sense. I didn't say anything at the time, but a few weeks later, I admitted to him I had figured it out. I spent the rest of the night assuring him I had no intention of telling another soul. It would have broken people in half to learn Tyler Parker liked guys, but as every woman knows as she gets older, the hot ones are always fucking gay.

"What did you do?" I asked before I had even closed the door.

He fell back into the oversized chair that was Kyle's favorite place to watch TV. I wasn't shocked to see a bottle covered by a paper bag in Tyler's hand, but I wasn't too thrilled with it either.

"Why do you automatically assume I did something?" I completely disliked that he took a good, long swallow of whatever bottle was hidden in the bag.

I am the last person to criticize someone for drinking too much. But in Tyler's case, when he started drinking that early in the day, he was headed for trouble, and he knew it. I drank more out of habit and because I didn't know how not to be drunk. Tyler drank when he was sad, angry, or both, and all alcohol did was make the situation worse. When we were still in high school, he had been picked up by the local police more times than anyone else we knew. Because he was a football star, the cops gave him a pass. I know that when he was in Florida, he had the same thing happen a few times, but again his status as a star football player gave him a level of immunity from the consequences.

After his knee got hurt, his protection was stripped away, and he ended up spending more than a few nights sobering up in a Foster jail cell.

104

He got better after his parents moved away. Running the sporting goods store had done him a world of good, but this thing with Matt looked like it was going to blow all the improvement out of the water.

"You're a man. Problems are always your fault," I joked.

"He's a man too, so why isn't it his fault?" he replied, trying to sound angry but ending up just coming across as miserable.

"Because I've known you too long, and this is about the time you start to throw wooden shoes into machinery," I answered plainly.

A few seconds later his head popped up. "Come again?"

"In the fifteenth century, workers used to wear wooden shoes called sabots. When they began to revolt, they threw their shoes into the machinery, hence the word sabotage," I said, trying to figure out if I had anything to actually eat in the house. If I wanted him to sober up, he needed food in his stomach.

He stared at me for almost thirty seconds before asking, "How the fuck do you know that?"

I shrugged, sitting across from him. "I know stuff." He continued to stare unbelievingly at me. "What? I do know stuff." More silence. "Fine, it's from one of Kyle's movies, but don't change the subject. What did you do?"

He hung his head. "I broke his window last night and didn't tell him." That caused me to pause for a moment. I knew he had been buzzed last night when he left, but breaking windows was new for Tyler. He saw the expression on my face and began to explain.

It was much worse than I thought.

Marvin Wallace

I like to think I was a good father to my three sons when they were growing up.

Of course, I'm sure Harry Truman thought he was a good president, but that just proves you're always the last person in a room to know you're an idiot.

I raised them all to be honest, brave, and above all else, to respect the people around them. A person never knows when he's going to need the kindness of strangers. I taught them how to shave, how to properly knot a tie, and I took each one out to learn the secrets of changing a flat tire in the middle of nowhere.

My oldest, John, assumed the responsibility of being the oldest boy the same way some men took to joining the Marines. Almost everything he did or said, he did with a seriousness that never failed to look five different types of cute in a boy of his age as he lectured and taught his younger brothers. John was the boy every father thinks he wants when they find out their wife is pregnant. He was a boy in every sense of the word, and I never once worried about him.

William, or Billy—the nickname he's never grown out of—is only a year and a half younger than John and has spent his entire life trying to be John. A few years back, I saw that Austin Powers movie on cable, and though it was nothing like the actual '60s, Mini-Me made me immediately think of Billy. If John had a Mini-Me, it would have been Billy. If John was lifting weights, Billy was there trying to lift as much. If he was under a car changing the oil, there was Billy right next to him, in the way. Every sports record John achieved was one Billy tried to beat, not a girl John liked that Billy didn't wink at, and not a stitch of clothing John owned that Billy didn't try to borrow. I never said anything aloud because when I say teenage boys have no humor about themselves at all, I learned from experience. My image of John and Billy is like a duckling waddling behind the mother duck, trying its hardest just to keep pace with it. I never worried about him either because I knew as long as John was flying straight, Billy was fine.

In comparison, there has never been a time I didn't worry about Matt.

People in this world say a lot of stupid things. Stuff like, if you support welfare you believe in socialism, if you disagree with the reasons we are in a war it means you are anti-American, and my favorite, being gay is a choice. As someone whose father survived the Great Depression only because of the assistance by the United States government, let me tell you, the only people who complain about federal welfare are the ones who have never needed it. As for war, I served my country for eight years active and another four reserve duty, and I am the most antiwar person you will ever meet. I did everything in my power to make sure my sons never had to answer that call, and if that makes me un-American, I dare you to come up and say it to my face.

As for being gay as a choice....

106

We knew Matt was different by the time he started kindergarten. I am in no way saying he was girly, but he was the least manly boy I had ever seen. Where kids his age lived for things like mud and bugs and farting, Matt would have none of it. He was fastidiously neat and did not care who could spit farther, pee longer, or run faster than anyone else. I wasn't sure at the time why he was so different, but when he hit puberty, it became clearer to me and his mother that the difference went deep. He tried too hard to be like his brothers and their friends. It wasn't an obvious thing. The only reason we noticed was when you watch a child from the first moment they open their eyes to the night they're standing in the hallway fumbling to put a corsage on a girl's wrist, there isn't much a parent doesn't know.

If you asked me when I was younger how I would react to one of my sons being gay, I can assure you more than a few curse words would have come up and the strong possibility of one of us limping away would have been in the cards. Instead, I found myself becoming more protective of Matt. I actually had to fight the constant urge to keep the world away from him because of the fear that it would turn its ignorant hatred to focus on him. I had to force myself to treat him exactly as I'd treated his brothers, but I watched and I worried. I shouldn't be so proud that my love for the boy never wavered for so much as a second, but I am.

But we always knew Matt was born that way.

We had grown used to the various shades of miserable that seemed to make up Matt's life over the years. It couldn't have been easy growing up in Foster with no one to talk to about being gay and what to do and all, so it came as no great shock that Matt tore out of town the second his high school diploma was placed in his hands. His mother was hurt, but she understood—this was not the place for him to find happy, and as parents, all you ever want is for your kids to be happy. The problem was that he was no happier in California than he had been in Foster. Every time we talked to him on the phone or saw him when he came home for Christmas, it was blatantly obvious the boy was as, if not more, miserable than he had been here.

And there was just no talking to him about it.

I know he is a grown man, but every time he rebuffed our attempts at trying to talk to him, all I saw was him at three insisting he was old enough to go to the potty by himself because he saw John and Billy doing it. Matt had backed himself into a bad corner. On one hand, he thought that if he admitted he needed help, he'd look less of a man than his other brothers. On the other hand, he couldn't wrap his mind around the fact that he was trying so hard and was still a sad person. John and Billy relished being able to cry on our shoulder when things went south, but not Matt. There were nights I lost sleep wondering if I had created an unobtainable model of masculinity by not acknowledging his sexuality, and only now were we seeing the results of that fucked-up choice.

And then Beth's friend Frances told her about her gay son and how miserable he was in Foster.

Everyone knew Tyler, of course. He rushed for over five hundred yards in one game his junior year and everything changed for him. Nearly every boy around these parts plays one sport or another growing up, but few are gifted with the talent that Tyler Parker showed on a hundred yards of green grass every Friday night. He was a good-looking young man who seemed to have the whole world ahead of him when he was eighteen.

And then lost all of it at nineteen.

I saw the game where his knee was blown out, and I am not ashamed to say there were tears in my eyes when he did not get up after that hit. The way he lay there, his arms clutching that one leg—there was no doubt what had happened, and I knew he was never going to play again. That Monday I saw the sporting goods store was closed, which meant the Parkers had flown out to Florida to check on their son. For a moment I thought I couldn't have been more miserable if one of my own sons had been hit. Then the thought of how it would feel to watch one of my boys not get up on national television and being aware that I was hours away from being able to help him hit me. I almost threw up on First Street.

Anyway, when my wife, Elizabeth, told me that Tyler had come out to his parents, I could see the little gears in her mind turn over and begin to spin. I tried to explain to her that to men, a mother's endorsement was not the grand slam she seemed to think it was. In fact, if my mother had tried to set me up on a date with Beth, I'm not so sure I wouldn't have turned it down completely out of spite. I imagine that it has something to do with dating eventually leading to sex, and no man alive wants his mother within fifty degrees of separation to the woman he's having relations with.

But after being married to her for almost forty years, let me assure you, I knew I had a better chance of deflecting a tornado with harsh words than I did of stopping Beth from doing what she wanted once she set her mind to it.

Suddenly my wife, who once referred to one of John's baseball uniforms as "his ball costume," was a regular at Parker's Sporting Goods store. This woman who could not tell me the difference between a touchdown and a home run was bringing home a variety of sports jerseys, two different beverage coolers, and once an athletic supporter complete with strap and cup. When I asked her about it, she said it was an investment in Matt's future and that she was saving all the receipts.

If you have never been married, let me give you some advice. Never stand between your spouse and whatever windmill they happen to be charging unless you feel like being knocked down and run over a few times. Beth had it in her mind that Tyler and Matt would work, and far be it from me to stop her.

Damned if she wasn't right.

Of course, she didn't have much to do about it in the scheme of things. They ran into each other over Christmas and hit things off, though maybe she had loosened the ketchup bottle that was Tyler's curiosity some, but life has a way of making things turn out the way they should.

This is all a long way of me saying that I had never seen Matt so happy in his life.

I can't say that the specifics of what those boys did when they were alone was all that appealing to me, but the fact that someone out there was making my boy feel good was more than enough for me. So when Matt came in from his run and rushed past us and upstairs like he was on fire, I was immediately concerned. That was old Matt behavior, and if old Matt was back, that could only mean one thing.

Beth took a few steps toward the stairs to follow him, but I waved her off. "Let me," I said, putting my newspaper down. "No boy wants to talk to his mother about his love life."

"Oh, and old men are their go-to choice?" she asked, even though she knew I was right.

"No. Children in general do not wish to discuss anything that involves a body part below the belt with their parents, but at the very least, another man can understand what a man is going through," I tried to assure her, but she wasn't buying it.

"Had a lot of gay relationships that didn't pan out?"

I waved a dismissive hand at her as I climbed the stairs. One, because I know that just pisses her off, but more so because I had absolutely no answer to that. I suppose she was right that when it came down to the mechanics of things, she might have more working knowledge of what having a relationship with a man is like, but she didn't know what I knew—how men think. Gay or not, Matt is still a man, and unless someone slipped him a how-to guide when he was in California, I bet he didn't know any better than I did how to make a relationship work.

I knocked on the door before I walked in, because I was the father of three sons, and over the years, I had walked in on more things I wished I could unsee than I care to share with anyone else. If you are a male, you know what I mean. If you have a son, you *really* know what I mean.

"What?" Matt's voice asked from the other side of the door.

"You decent?" I asked, pausing for a few seconds in case he wasn't. "Because I'm coming in."

The door swung open and he stood there, trying his best not to look mad. He failed pretty badly, but bless him for at least trying. "I didn't go by Nancy's." I stood there not knowing what the hell he was talking about. "I'll call about the window in a few."

Right, the window. Because that was the only thing around here broken.

"Ain't no hurry," I replied, walking into the room. On the bed was his suitcase, which pretty much confirmed what I had already feared. "Going somewhere?"

"Home," he answered, going back to the closet and grabbing a handful of clothes. "Work called, and they need me back."

Matt was a bright boy and was very good at many things. Lying was not one of them.

"They called you, huh?" I asked, sitting on the edge of the bed. He nodded as he went back for another handful. "I must be falling behind with the technology these days," I commented, sounding as nonchalant as I could muster. "Here I always thought you needed a phone on you to get a call." He stopped and looked at me in confusion, and then saw I was pointing to the cell phone on the nightstand. "You wanna try best two out of three?"

He shoved the clothes into his suitcase without a word. He'd inherited the silent response from me. When we had nothing in way of a comeback, we just fumed silently and hoped the rage radiating off us would work as a repellent. Matt's rage might work on other people but never on me.

"So you're leaving? Just like that?" I asked, already knowing the answer.

He opened the top drawer, took an armful of socks and underwear out, and deposited them on top of the clothes already overflowing from the suitcase. "I've been here too long as it is," he shot back, his voice full of hurt and anger that had nothing to do with me. "I have a life, Dad."

"Do you?" He froze as those two words slammed into his funk and brought it to a grinding halt. "What happened between you and Tyler?" I asked, cutting through this nonsense, trying to get to what was really wrong.

"I do have a life," he repeated, ignoring my question altogether. "I know you and Mom don't think there is anything of value outside of Foster, but there is and I'm happy there!" He wasn't talking to me anymore. His words were the only way he knew to convince himself. "I am happy out there!" I stayed silent. "I *am*!" More silence.

When he saw I wasn't going to react, his voice cracked. When a parent has ushered three boys through the perils of childhood into the world of manhood, the signs when one of them is about to fall apart are clear. I cleared the short distance between me and him as he began to cry.

"I fucked things up, Dad" was all he got out before he lost it.

There are few things males will admit out loud because we're all so caught up in trying to be men that we're unable to get over it and tell the truth. At times like this, when the very world itself looks like it has turned against you, there is nothing a boy wants more than his father to just hold him and whisper in his ear that everything is going to be all right.

From personal experience, as a man gets older, if his father has already passed on, his wife makes a more than an acceptable substitute, but don't tell Beth that. It'll just go to her head.

Kyle

I have a weird life.

I don't say that in a poor-me kind of way so I come off like some orphan from a Dickens novel. Pity is one of those things like a pet rock or one of those stupid birds that drink water out of a glass. People think other people want it, but if you were to take a poll, no one would ever ask for it. I am more making an observation that my life, when held up against other lives, is fracking weird.

For example.

When I left this morning, my mother was passed out in her room, and the living room looked like one of those crime scenes you see on a CSI show, the one where there's a chalk outline where the body isn't. You know what I mean, right? With the bottles all over the place, discarded cigarette butts near the bottles, and a small mirror that had to have been cleaned with baby powder because there is no other earthly reason for it to have white powder on it, right?

I kid. I know what the white powder was.

Anyway, the only thing missing was a dead whore in the middle of the room and that weird track lighting I assume comes with all hotel rooms in Vegas. There are mornings I walk out of my bedroom and expect to hear the Who start to play as I walk into the bathroom, just to warn me what the rest of the place looks like. Normally the whole messed-up living room and mother passed out in her bedroom thing wouldn't have pissed me off as much as it did. Except she had promised me she was going to change.

The "she" in that sentence being my mom, and change meaning not what had happened last night.

She had really come through for Brad when they tried to kick him off the baseball team last month, and since then it really looked like she was going to change. Of course, like the idiot monkey that always touches the electrified button, I believed her and thought things were looking up.

Long story short, I was wrong and there was nothing anyone could do about it.

So I decided to use a lifeline and phoned a friend. Well, in this case, I phoned a boyfriend and got a hot jock delivered to my door. I am, of course, bragging, because I knew this was how other people saw him but not me. I knew who he really was now, so every time I looked at him, I saw the small things that made me crazy instead of the glaring, obvious ones that made everyone else lust after him.

Take, for example, the way his hair always looks on the verge of being messy. It's adorable, I mean just drop-dead cute as hell, and to the outside observer, must look like when he rolls out of bed. I see it and I smile about the thirty-plus minutes I know he spent in the bathroom with a handful of product trying to get it to look *just* messy enough to look random but good enough to make him that much more attractive. The way his white T-shirt hugs him so casually, showing off his broad chest without being as obvious as wearing a fitted shirt might—to everyone else, he looks as if he threw one on and ran out the door. The truth was that he bought the shirts a size too small and spent a week washing and stretching them to look that haphazard on purpose.

People see an insanely hot guy who looks like that without any effort at all. I see the self-conscious guy behind the curtain making sure as many people like him as possible. And if they aren't going to like him, at least they will admit he is handsome. I'm sure it sounds vain to you, but I assure you it is as fear-based as anything else we do to make ourselves presentable to the public. The only difference is that those of us who are normal-looking don't have a bar to reach when we walk out the door. So my hair is shaggy, my jeans frayed. Who cares? I mean, before I came out, no one knew who the hell I was anyway. I could have shown up with a Pokémon shirt and bell-bottoms and no one would have noticed. People *do* notice him, and Brad knows it, and for some reason he is terrified of coming up short.

And for some reason, I find that fear in someone who so doesn't need to work so hard at being hot is irresistible.

So when he pulled up wearing a ball cap and his letterman jacket, I knew he literally ran out the door to get me out of there. And if that wasn't worth melting over a little, I don't know what is.

I left the house in a state of disarray but without dead bodies evident. When I came back after lunch to see if my mother had crawled out of her cave, the living room looked cleaned up, but there was a dead body on the couch.

See what I mean? Weird.

At first, I had no idea who the corpse in question was. Because it lay facedown in the cushions, all I could see was that he was a full-grown man and he had a nice ass. I know that makes me sound like a perv crushing on some old dead guy, but I assure you, some asses transcend age, and this was one of them. I wasn't aware my mom knew anyone with that nice a body; if I had, I would have been nicer to him. I inched closer to make sure I was just being sarcastic and the guy was really breathing when he snorted in his sleep and turned over to face me.

Holy shit, it was Mr. Parker!

You'd think he was some hideous monster the way I jumped back, but he was anything but. From what I had gathered from my mom, he'd been some kind of high school football star who ended up busting his knee out his first season at college and had to come back to Foster for some reason or another. I couldn't imagine anything worse than that. I mean, bad enough he'd worked his ass off—again with his ass! Man, I need to focus—and actually got out of *Matrix Four: The Mayberry Years*, but to end up being sent back here had to be on par with finding out the golden ticket you found in your chocolate bar was really just a cheap-ass coupon, and by the way, you and your freeloading grandfather can get back on the bus and enjoy a lifetime of cabbage soup.

Okay, maybe it wasn't like that for him, but I damn well know if it was me, I'd be wishing some pain on the next fat-faced blueberry chick I saw.

He was handsome in a way that was just wrong on someone his age. Not that he was, like, ancient or anything, but he was as old as my mom, and by that time the slope down to ancient gets pretty slippery. More times than not, folks my mom and Mr. Parker's age just look old. Not Mr. Parker. He looked like one of those stupid, hot jocks all grown up with adult clothes on. "Adult clothes" here meaning their pants are actually at their waist and stuff. Brad thought the guy hung the moon, which made me jealous for about five seconds. Then I realized this guy had played against Brad's dad when they were in high school, and there isn't a guy who would find his dad hot, even with a gun pointed at his head.

Though he didn't say anything, I think Mr. Parker had talked to Brad about us at some point, which made the man a superhero in my book. The fact my mom and him were, like, best friends from high school just made the microscopic size of this town all the more apparent to me. The day he stood up for Brad, and I guess me too, at the school board meeting was the day I realized being gay wasn't automatically a death sentence.

"Bitch please," a voice said from the chair.

Sighing I turned at looked at Billy, who was not a real person but a personification of all my negative thoughts boiled into one annoying manifestation. Confused? How do you think I feel?

"You don't think they know who I am?"

I wish I didn't know who he was.

"Okay that's low, and you're being overly dramatic. *Again.*"

"Whatever," I said, sitting on the small love seat. "I thought being gay was going to be horrible. Wander around with a big scarlet letter on my chest, being shunned wherever I went. So yeah, compared to that, death would seem a kindness."

Billy was looking as its nails, bored. "You done? Great, my turn."

Billy got up and started to pace the room. "One, you aren't that stupid. You have cable, you know there are other gay people in the world. Two, if you think this man is a sign that you're going to turn out okay, then think again."

"What's wrong—"

Billy held up a finger. "Not done."

I shut up.

"And three...." Billy trailed off. "You're stupid."

I cracked a grin. "You didn't have a three; you just wanted to interrupt me."

Billy rolled his eyes and sat back down.

"What's wrong with him?" I asked.

"What's not? Look at him, I mean really look at him. He's old as fuck, he ain't ugly, and he's single. Now what does that tell you?"

"Um, he's a handsome middle-aged man who happens to be single?"

"No!" Billy snapped. "It means he has to be trouble, or he'd be with someone already."

Hmmm, I hadn't thought of that.

Well okay, I obviously did since Billy did, but I haven't had the thought out loud yet. What was wrong with him? A guy like that should be able to chuck a rock and find someone to date. I mean, if I can get a guy like Brad, this guy should be able to score anyone he wants.

"So then why he is dead on our couch?" Billy asked.

It was a good question.

I resisted the urge to find a stick and poke him with it, something I had wanted to do to a dead body since I had seen *Stand by Me*. Instead, I went to the kitchen and made some coffee. I may only be seventeen, but I had a doctorate in dealing with drunks. I was the freaking Doogie Howser of enabling, and I knew what a Budweiser nap looked like from this distance. I also knew how to counter it.

Two parts caffeine, which was the coffee, one part pain relief, which was the aspirin I was grabbing, apply cold water, in this case a damp washcloth, and speak very, very softly. In this case that would be, "Mr. Parker? Are you awake?" Which was what you asked, even though you knew the person wasn't. I am not sure when this whole line of counterintuitive questions became the norm, but I know if I was passed out like that, someone asking me if I was awake would just piss me the hell off.

"Mr. Parker," I tried again, this time poking his shoulder. "Are you awa—"

His hand snapped out and grabbed my wrist so fast, I swore I could hear that martial arts movie break as one eye stared up at me. In a voice barely above a growl, he asked, "Kyle? Why are you in my house?"

I tried to pull my hand back slowly, but there was no way I was getting it back unless he let go.

"Wow," I exclaimed, looking at the complete lack of effort he was exerting holding me tight. "You are crazy strong."

His gaze followed mine to his hand, and just like that, I was free. It took some effort not to go stumbling backward like a spaz, but I managed.

"Sorry," he rattled off, not sounding the least bit sorry. "Now why the fuck are you in my house?"

I set the coffee down on the table in front of him. "Um, you wanna try that again?" I asked, making sure I was more than an arm's length away from him before I spoke.

He began to sit up and then cried out like he'd been shot. I saw his hands move over his head, and it looked like he was trying to hold his skull together, which did nothing to deter from the visual that he had just been tagged by Lee Harvey Oswald taking a left turn on Houston.

"Coffee in front of you, bottle of aspirin next to it," I said, making sure my voice never got above what I had determined was a drunk person's pain threshold when spoken to. As he blindly reached out for the cup, I swore to myself I was never going to drink alcohol. Never ever.

"Little to the right," I coached, since he missed the table entirely the first three times.

On the fourth he grabbed the cup and pulled it to his lips, looking way too much like Gollum from *The Lord of the Rings*. The way he cradled the coffee and sipped? I kid you not; if he said "My precious," I might have just turned and run. After a few tentative swallows, he popped open the aspirin and downed a handful as if they were candy and then lay back down on the couch, putting the washcloth over his eyes.

"Thank you," he croaked.

"All part of the service here at the Days Inn," I mumbled as I sat back and watched him lie there. After about a minute, he looked out from under the washcloth and glanced over at me. I waved at him. "Hi, still here."

Sighing, he covered his eyes again and asked, "Where's Brad?"

"Not dead on my couch," I answered quickly. Then I started laughing, because all I could hear in my head was Quentin Tarantino asking if there was a sign outside that said Dead Gay Guy Storage. Mr. Parker gave me a weird look—no, he gave me a look like I was weird, and I laughed more loudly. "Sorry, pop culture junkie. So… this about the guy you've been seeing?" I asked as bluntly as I could.

117

If he had been a cartoon, his jaw would have dropped and then fallen off his face.

"How did you…," he began to say, and then his brain caught up. "Did your mom…?" He stopped again. "How did you…?" He started again. I think I broke Mr. Parker.

"Um, Brad told me he saw you with a guy, one of the Allman brothers?" I explained, a little fuzzy on the last part.

"Wallace brothers," he corrected me, sounding like he was mortified.

"Right, them. He said you looked happy, which he made sound like it was not a normal way for you to look. So I assumed it meant you guys had met after all and were… dating? Hooking up? Something?" I thought about that for a moment. "Unless it was with another guy and just an internet thing. In that case, it was probably about sex and you wouldn't want to talk about that at all, which is understandable." I looked up at him, knowing this was killing him. "Was it just a sex thing, Mr. Parker?"

Truth? I knew this was about what he was rambling about when he came into Nancy's a few weeks ago. I didn't need to be Sherlock Holmes to put that together. And I knew it wasn't just a sex thing. In fact, I wasn't sure guys that old still had sex, much less sex on the internet. I knew Brad's mom had Facebook, which had to be the worst thing in the world since she practically made him add her as a friend, but besides that I didn't know any sites old people used to hook up. So honestly, all I was doing was busting his balls, because it really looked like he was in a bad place and a little humor never hurt anyone.

"No," he answered hoarsely. Realizing how bad he sounded, he took another sip of coffee. "It wasn't a sex thing," he admitted after a while.

"So then where is the Allman brother?"

"Wallace, his name is Matt Wallace," he corrected me.

"So then where is Matt?" I asked him point-blank.

He ran a hand through his hair, which is something Brad did when he couldn't think of what to say and was stalling for time. "We… well, he… he's leaving," he decided on.

What he said and what he meant were obviously two different things. What he said was, "He's leaving." What he meant was, "He's leaving *me*." I don't like to brag, but I speak fluent silence.

Now, here is one of the many differences between me and other guys my age. Most guys would have been all "aw shucks" about dealing with an adult as an equal and just talking to him. Most guys my age see adults as these weird aliens who say they used to be kids way back in the Stone Age but have no real memory of their time spent as "teenagers" so spout this crap they call wisdom that does absolutely nothing to help in the long run. They aren't like the parents in the Peanuts cartoons where they speak in this weird language no one understands; they're more like statues that just stand there in curious poses and dare us to decipher what they're trying to say. Let me tell you, after about ten minutes playing Pictionary with a statue, you'll walk away shaking your head, wondering why you even tried in the first place.

I don't see adults like that.

The adults I have interacted with in my long seventeen years of life have all struck me as being the same kind of person I was, only they had more experience at pretending to know what they were talking about. I mean, that's the only difference, if you break it down. They have the same fears and the same worries that we do; they've just had time to build up this invisible shell around them that makes them seem like it doesn't affect them at all. So in comparison, kids end up looking like we are one Red Bull away from an epileptic fit every time we encounter something outside our comfort zone.

But inside, they're just as fucked-up as we are.

"So he's leaving and you're okay with that," I said distantly, as if I were mulling it over in my head. "I can understand that. I mean, with all the single men in Foster, why tie yourself down to just one guy? And it's not like he's cute as fuck and seems to like you too, so you dodged a bullet on that one." I looked back at him and gave him the most sincere expression I could muster up. "I mean, as a burgeoning gay teenager, these are the life lessons I should take away from this, right?"

His eyes narrowed in suspicion as he carefully put down the coffee cup. "Does Brad know you're an evil genius underneath all that hair?"

Grinning back, I said, "In his defense, he does know it and accepts that one day I might end up taking over the world, but don't change the subject. If you like this guy and he's leaving, why aren't you stopping him?"

I don't know who was more shocked that he didn't have an answer, him or me.

"I have to go," he said, standing up quickly. "I need…." He started patting his pockets down. "My keys." He looked around the room in a panic.

We searched for ten minutes before I found them stuck in the cushions of my TV chair. I tossed them to him. "Go get him, Mr. Parker."

He almost sprinted out my door. "Thank you, and Kyle?" he asked as he opened the door. "Try to be a benevolent ruler when you take over."

I shrugged. "I'll consider it."

He laughed as he slammed the door and ran to his car.

Grown-ups! What can you do about them?

TYLER

I REMEMBER my dad used to have a bumper sticker that read "Teenagers, move out now while you know everything!" When I was a teenager, I thought it was insulting; as I got older, I thought it was fitting, and finally, lately, I found it funny. After talking to Kyle, I'm not so sure that bumper sticker was wrong. If I'd had my head on as tight at seventeen as that kid seemed to at his age, I would... well, I'd probably be ruling the world myself. I could tell Kyle was a special guy when we'd talked at Nancy's, but after that little sparring match at Linda's, I understood more what Brad saw in him.

One of the only advantages of living in a town the size of Foster is that someone can get to anywhere from anywhere within five minutes if you know how to avoid the lights. When I pulled up in front of the Wallace house, I could see the rental car Matt had been driving was gone, and I felt my stomach lurch in fear. I ran up to the door and started banging on it, a little louder than I intended because I heard a scream of, "Marvin! They're back!" which made no sense to me.

Matt's dad swung open the door, a scowl on his face and a shotgun in his hand.

"Whoa!" I said, holding up my hands as I took a step back. "Mr. Wallace, it's me! Tyler!"

"It's just the Parker boy!" he shouted into the house, leaning the shotgun against the door frame before he opened the screen door. "He's gone, son. He left about twenty minutes ago for the airport."

I felt like throwing up.

"What happened between you two?" he asked with real sadness in his voice. "I thought you guys were good together."

So a teenage kid and now a grandfather told me they could see something from afar that I had been blind to this whole time.

"I screwed up," I admitted, feeling like sitting down and never getting up again.

"No," he countered slowly. "You're *screwing* it up. Game isn't over until the clock stops."

I nodded and looked up at the sky in an effort to keep my tears in my eyes and not running down my face. I had no idea what Mr. Wallace was talking about.

He sighed, reached up, and grabbed the front of my shirt. He hauled me down to eye level with him and talked in the same way you'd explain to a small child or a very slow adult. "You haven't screwed it up. You are screwing it up as we speak." I blinked in confusion. "Oh dear God! He's probably still at the airport! If you hurry you can catch him before his flight takes off. Get a move on!"

I had given up on Matt twice without even trying. There wasn't going to be a third time.

"Thank you, Mr. Wallace!" I called out, running back to my car as fast as I could.

I saw him roll his eyes as he made "move it!" motions with his free hand.

I had a plane to catch.

MATT

HOW SAD is it I keep expecting him to show up?

Personally, I blame *Pretty Woman*. If a billionaire can fall in love with a call girl and come for her, then surely I have to rate at least one rescue? Of course, Tyler showing up would depend on him knowing I was leaving on this particular flight. Since I hadn't called him, unless Tyler was psychic, I was out of luck.

Not that I had squirreled away a huge amount of luck so far, but however small my stockpile was, it was now gone.

The worst part was that I couldn't even blame this on bad luck, since the odds of me running into him, him being gay, and him liking me were the statistical equivalent of winning three Powerball lotteries back to back. Fate had tossed a perfect sixty-yard Hail Mary right into my numbers, and I'd dropped the ball. I mean, what else could I do with that perfectly tossed pigskin *but* drop it? People like me weren't meant to be happy. We were too sad, too gloomy for normal people to handle on an extended basis. Sophia had told me repeatedly—I wore my sorrow like a raincoat, and no matter how sunny a day might be, there I was, always ready for rain.

I waited at the rental car place for a good ten minutes, hoping he'd show up.

When I heard my flight called on the PA, I sighed to myself quietly and made my way to the gate. When the clerk handed me my boarding pass, I felt like she was handing me a death sentence of sorts. I was being sentenced to life—a life spent alone and miserable.

I said nothing as I took it and plodded down the Jetway to my flight.

TYLER

I'VE HEARD a lot of complaints about the changes to the world since 9/11; most of the time, I ignored them.

Showing up hours before a flight sucks, and no one likes taking their shoes off while going through security, but I never really had a problem with those restrictions. In fact, I was pro airline security so far, because I didn't like much thinking about the consequences if we didn't do all that. Right until I needed to get to Matt.

Turns out, no one likes a full-grown man running into an airport making a mad dash toward the security gate like he was on fire.

It honestly hadn't even occurred to me that I wouldn't be able to get to Matt once I made it to the terminal. I had this whole image of catching him just as he boarded his flight, turning him around, and giving him a kiss so strong he'd swoon into my arms. I'm talking a full-blown dip-and-bend-your-knees kind of kiss that you lose time in because you're holding your breath during it.

I did not imagine having two TSA guards eyeing me like I had a shoe full of explosives. Did that guy have a shoe full of explosives? Is that what happened? Now that I think about it, how do you use a shoe bomb without blowing your foot off? Well, I guess if your plot is to take a plane down, you aren't worried about your foot.

But still, a bomb in your foot?

I stood at the windows watching his flight taxi toward the runway. His phone kept going to voicemail while I watched him leave my life, probably forever. Linda was right—I was just a chickenshit. I always had, in the back of my mind, a tried-and-true escape clause. I'd do something to push him away so I never had to actually face the fact that I was gay and wanted to spend my life with a guy. A small, thin voice inside my head kept telling me if I just waited, someday I'd be normal. I'd used the voice's logic to escape in high school, I used it with Riley, and I was using it at that moment in the airport.

Except—

When I saw his plane take off, returning Matt to San Francisco and me to Alone, I realized I didn't want to be normal.

"Fuck this," I said to myself while I dialed Linda's number.

"Tyler? Where did you go?" she asked, clearly worried.

"Dallas. Can you check on Brad? He's taking over the shop for a while," I said, digging through my wallet.

"I can, but where are you going?" She sounded as confused as I felt.

I handed my credit card to the girl behind the ticket counter. "Next flight to San Francisco, please," I said to her before going back to Linda. "I'm going to go get him. The keys to the shop are on my key chain. Would you mind asking Brad and Kyle to make sure the shop's taken care of while I'm gone? Brad knows what to do."

"Tyler," she cautioned. "Slow down a second."

The ticket agent handed me my card and boarding pass. "I'm tired of slowing down. I'm tired of being scared. I'm sick of being like this. Linda, I need to get him back."

I had to sound like a lunatic to the people around me and to Linda as well.

"What if he doesn't want to come back?" she asked quietly.

"Then I sit outside his house until he decides to take me back." The TSA guy gestured for me to put my phone into the plastic tub before I walked through the metal detector. "I have to go, Linda. Wish me luck."

I could hear the smile in her voice. "Go get him, then."

I hung up the phone and vowed to do just that.

MATT

THERE IS a bone-crushing sorrow that happens in airports.

If anything in the world can drive home the fact you are alone, it's watching other people walking off an airplane, down a Jetway, and through a terminal until they spot a cheering crowd of loved ones. At first they walk slowly, stretching out tight muscles and hauling in uncanned air. Then, after a pause to figure out which way the exit is, they start toward the people who are waiting for them. By the time those folks are visible, the new arrival is practically running and smiling from ear to ear.

We walk through life with these social walls that keep people out of our lives the best we can. We keep our voices down, our expressions of emotion muted in respect for the strangers around us.

Those walls come crumbling down at airports for some reason.

A soldier, no older than twenty-two, had been a few people ahead of me as we disembarked the plane. He had an Army-green bag in one hand as he tried to push past or eel around people in the most respectful way he could manage. The moment he broke free of the crowd, he dropped the bag and dashed into the arms of a blonde girl who had been cleared as far as the gate and who was openly crying at just the sight of him. He lifted and spun her around as if she weighed nothing. I seriously doubted if anything this side of a nuclear war could part their lips.

It was such an unabashed expression of love that it affected everyone who saw it. People smiled; I saw some sigh in longing. I felt the hole in the center of my soul grow larger as the fact no one was here for me settled in, instantly coupled with the realization no one would ever be waiting for me like that. Ever.

I looked away from the young couple and tried not to resent their love too much as I walked to baggage claim.

While I waited for our flight's luggage to be unloaded, I stared around, puzzled by something that was hard to identify at first. The entire world seemed different to me. The light looked harsher than normal, my limbs weighed more than they usually did, and I felt as if I had just run a marathon and was at the end of my endurance. The people looked flat, expressionless, two-dimensional to me. As I scanned the crowd in apathy, my world was painted with varying shades of sadness. Nothing caught my attention except that grayness; nothing, not even the color, mattered.

Was this what the rest of my life was going to be like?

I grabbed my bags and caught a taxi to my place. The city blurred by me. Part of me looked for something that would trigger my interest, bring back a memory. But everything kept on looking the same—gray, lifeless, and foreign to me. I honestly didn't recognize my apartment building when we pulled up in front of it. It took the driver calling out, "Hey!" twice to get my attention. "We're here," he said when I looked back at him.

"So we are," I mumbled to myself as I tossed some bills at him.

"This is way too much," he called after me when I got out of the cab.

I didn't even answer. I carried my bags, which weighed more and more and pulled me toward the floor with each step.

I walked up to the third floor with the same reluctance with which a condemned man walks to the gallows. I wanted to collapse on the stairs and stop moving, but the desire to hide in my bed under the covers and never emerge was stronger. As I opened the door, the stale air of my living room hit me. It didn't smell the way I remembered the air in my apartment smelling. All signs of my being there had faded over the weeks I'd been gone. I might as well have been walking into my home for the first time.

This was home now.

The suitcases fell out of my hands as that thought hit the still waters of my mind and slowly sank below the surface. I was never going to go back to Foster again. Seeing Tyler again would be akin to crawling naked through three miles of broken glass just so I could roll around in Tabasco sauce for an hour after. I kicked the door closed behind me and stumbled to my bed. I fell forward, no doubt looking like a great gay tree that had been cut at its roots.

I lay there not moving for a few minutes before I heard the beep. I ignored the sound, but a few minutes later it repeated itself. I looked over to the digital answering machine and saw its one red eye blinking back at me. It would beep every few minutes until I checked the messages. No matter how hard I stared at it, the machine refused to explode. Sighing, I got up off the bed and walked over to the offensive device. I pushed the Replay button.

"Matt," my mom's voice asked over the machine, "are you there? You aren't answering your phone. Call me when you get home, please." A small beep signaled that the machine had erased the message. The next one chimed in. "Matthew, this isn't funny. Your mother is worried. Answer your phone!" my father's voice scolded me as if he could make me hear his command through sheer force of will alone. Another beep and Sophia's crone-like voice issued from the speaker. "Hey, fag, I think you lost your phone somewhere. I just called it and a seriously gay flight attendant answered. Normally I would think you might be getting lucky, but this guy was making Jack from *Will & Grace* look like John Wayne. Anyway, call me when you get this. Unless you *are* doing the flight steward. In that case, get an old priest and a young priest and pray." Her laugh made me shiver with the same revulsion I felt when a fork scraped across a metal skillet. Thankfully the machine cut her off. Another beep.

I cursed to myself as I turned on my computer.

A normal person would have been pissed, or at the very least, annoyed by the loss of a cell phone, but for me, it was relaxing. In a sea of things I had no control over, finding my phone was the one small piece of wood I could cling to. I opened the browser and pinged my number.

It was less than a mile away and moving toward me.

"What the—?" I asked out loud as I pinged the phone again.

It was closer.

Something was wrong. Unless it had developed wings and a homing device, my phone couldn't be coming toward me. Unless someone was bringing it to me. Maybe the airline had a service? I had flown first class, and it wasn't hard to check a smartphone for its home address. The dot on my computer stopped in front of my apartment. Less than a minute later, someone buzzed for me to unlock the entry door downstairs.

I pushed the Admit buzzer so whoever it was could come up and pulled my wallet out to see how much cash I had on me. There was no way the guy who had followed me home from the airport was getting paid enough for the service. I had two ones and a twenty. I thought about it for a few seconds and took the twenty out.

I opened the door on the first knock. "Thanks, you're a lifesaver…," I said, holding out the money.

Tyler stood there, my phone in his hand.

TYLER

As soon as we landed in Phoenix, I tried to find a faster connecting flight. Matt had complained that he couldn't get a direct flight out of Dallas home; he was going to have to stop twice and change planes once. So I had a small chance of catching him.

Normally, I am not one to lean on my looks, but in times of crisis, I have found that my smile can open a few doors. It had no effect on the ladies at the Delta and Southwest counters, but the guy at the American terminal was a whole different story. He had glanced up and given me a perfunctory nod before going back to his computer.

I thought I was screwed until his head popped back up to give me a second look.

"Can I help you?" he asked, with more emphasis on the word "help" than he probably intended. He cleared his throat and added quickly, "I mean, did you need some assistance?"

I smiled at him and saw him swallow slightly. He had just been clocked, and worse, he knew he had been clocked. "I need to get to San Francisco," I said, walking closer to the counter. "I need to be there as soon as possible."

He slowly looked away from me as he began to push keys on the computer in front of him. "So… family emergency?" he asked, looking down at the screen for a few seconds and then back at me.

I thought about leading this guy on to find a flight, but it just wasn't in me. I sighed and leaned into the counter. "Look, I met this great guy and I completely screwed it up and he's on his way to San Francisco and I need to get there to beg him to take me back. Can you please help me?" I will admit, I gave him puppy dog eyes, but I was truly desperate.

I could hear his typing slow down as I admitted I was chasing a guy.

"Please," I began to babble. "You have to know how hard it is to find a real guy in this world, and if you found one and screwed it up… wouldn't you want someone like you to help me out?"

130

We held eye contact, neither one of us even drawing a breath, like two gay gunslingers staring each other down. Finally he sighed and looked back at the computer. "If I had a guy looking like you running after me, I would make sure to trip and let you catch up." He pushed a few more buttons. "There's a nonstop leaving in about ten minutes from gate twenty-two," he said, gesturing with his head. "If you hurry, I am sure you can exchange your ticket. They have room."

"Bless you!" I said, resisting the urge to lean over the counter and give him a kiss.

"Whatever," he said, smiling. "But my name is Shawn, and if he turns you down, I work here Tuesday through Saturday every week."

I gave him a wink. "Thanks." I ran as fast as I could to gate twenty-two.

The lady at the gate began to hassle me about the flight until I mentioned Shawn had sent me. She gave me a glance from head to toe and then scoffed quietly. "That figures." She pushed a few buttons herself. "Okay, I can get you on. But I only have first class. Credit card?"

I handed it over to her, and a few minutes and several hundred dollars later, I sat in a seat in the back of first class. My heart was racing so fast I thought there was no way I would even close my eyes on the flight, but somewhere over Oklahoma, I passed out. I had a dream I was talking to Matt, but every time I tried to answer his questions, my mouth refused to work and I struggled to speak. He finally shook his head in disgust and turned away from me. I tried to grab at him, but something was holding me back. I looked down and saw a mass of people pulling at me, at my clothes, dragging me away from Matt. Everyone I knew in Foster, the entire town, was bent on dragging me down into the ground. Matt got farther and farther away. I sank into nothing.

I woke up screaming.

That doesn't sound so bad, but inside a locked airplane at 33,000 feet, it is considered kind of a thing. There were two attendants and the air marshal standing by me when I finally came out of my delirium. I had a very strong feeling I was a couple of minutes away from being tased. "Problem?" I asked, realizing I had been drooling in my sleep.

The air marshal looked at me, his hand still by his stun gun. "You tell us, son."

"You were yelling in your sleep," the lady next to me said to me in a concerned voice.

"We going to have a problem?" the marshal asked, sounding more like an Old West cowboy than a twenty-first-century law officer.

I resisted the urge to ask him whether or not we'd step outside if I did have a problem. Instead I just shook my head. "Bad dream, I'm sorry."

He gave me that lingering eye all cops seem to learn somewhere along the line. Like he was going to spin back and catch me rubbing my hands and laughing manically when I thought he was looking away. "We land in thirty minutes," he said to me. "Make sure I don't have to walk up here again."

Again, I forced down the sarcastic comeback and watched him walk away.

Since there was no way I could sleep after that, I sat up and tried to compose my thoughts a little. The plan in my mind had consisted of three simple steps. Step one, get to California as fast as I could. Step two, get Matt back. Step three, Matt and I live happily ever after. Step one was about to become a reality, which left step two. Let me assure you, I may have a bit of an inflated opinion of my looks, but I knew there was no way in hell I could just smile my way back into Matt's life. I had screwed up, and that meant more than a cocky grin was going to be required to clean up the mess.

The question in my mind at that point was, did I have enough of anything to fix what I'd done? Or was really fixing it going to take more than I possessed?

My main asset in life so far had been my body, and to deny it would be ludicrous. I wasn't a Rhodes Scholar; the words in my head were never going to change the world in any noticeable way. I never graduated college, so I didn't have success as other people judged it. I ran the only sporting goods store in a small town and that was it. I was on the wrong side of thirty and not getting any younger. No matter how much I tried to stay in shape, I continued to age just like everyone else.

Matt was smart, successful, and still looked as good if not better than he had in high school. As the plane landed, I added up the pluses and minuses on my mental list and realized there was no logical reason for him to change his life for me. I was one of those pathetic people whose best days were in high school; life after that went into a constant downward spiral. Who would want to date a guy like me? What was the point?

As the plane nosed up, dropped flaps, and started its final approach, I wondered what I was doing on a plane about to land in San Francisco. All my drive and desire to get here had fled, leaving me feeling like a fraud, just another dummy pretending to be a real boy and not even doing that well. I sat there silently as the rest of the passengers disembarked, wondering what I should do.

"Sir," the attendant said to me. "Sir, we've arrived." The air marshal was standing behind her.

I honestly thought about starting something just so I could get arrested and have a reason not to go see Matt. Instead, I nodded and shuffled off the plane, wondering where my feet were taking me since my mind had no idea.

It turns out my feet thought I needed a drink, since I ended up in an airport bar ordering a double of anything strong. I nursed the drink as I tried not to think of what to do next. I had made good time here; in fact, I was pretty sure Matt's plane had landed less than a half hour before mine, since he'd had two layovers. If I ran, there was a chance I might catch him at baggage claim.

Instead, I just took another sip and started to smooth the ruffled fur of the depression I had long since embraced.

"Long day?" a voice asked from my right. I looked over and saw my Ghost of Christmas Yet to Come sitting next to me. He was maybe six or seven years older than I was and wearing a suit that would have looked old 30,000 miles ago. His hand gripped the tumbler of brown liquor tightly, as if he was trying to make sure it wouldn't shake. His smile was genuine, but his breath reeked of desperation along with the alcohol in a way that made something inside me cringe away.

I take that back—he wasn't desperate. He was just lonely.

His smile revealed his entire life to me. He was past fifty, never settled down, and was losing a fight with his waistline no matter how hard he battled against it. He had enjoyed a handful of lovers but had never found one love. He probably used his job, which consisted of a lot of travel, as the main reason for his lack of a lasting relationship, but the truth was, he knew there was something part shark inside him, and if it stopped swimming, looking for its next meal, it and he would quietly die. The job was a good excuse at thirty, less so, but still somewhat understandable, at forty. But at fifty, the way he lived wasn't about his work, and it wasn't about the guys he had dated.

It was about him.

The thing about knowing you're broken is that knowing is not enough to fix it. He had no idea why he had never settled down. No one really knows. It all came down to if you felt like a slut or a commitment-phobe, because there wasn't any empirical evidence to support either choice.

So he goes through life knowing he's sick but not knowing what to take to cure himself. In lieu of a metaphorical medicine, he's taken any and all remedies that have crossed his path. Younger men or friends with benefits are just snake oils and electrical devices he's used and uses to try to make himself feel better. More and more he medicated the symptoms rather than finding the actual cause.

What I am trying to say is that he ended up drinking a lot.

That was why his hand was so tightly gripped around his drink. He had been in meetings all day, and there in the bar at the airport was the first time he'd had to stop and have a real drink, so he was getting close to his limit. There were the headaches combined with the shakes, which were his body's way of reminding him it had been far too long since he'd tried to slowly kill the pain. He was waiting for a flight but would cancel it and fly out tomorrow if I gave him the nod. We'd spend the night in a hotel room where his fucking would be hard and savage, not because that was the way he liked it but because he was mad at himself for giving in to his desires again.

The bed would be destroyed as we lay there covered in a fine sheen of sweat, both of us staring up at the ceiling, each of us wondering why we had just done what we'd done. The euphoric high that comes from shooting a load would drift away, leaving us with the ugly reality that the other person was still in the room. He would get up and shuffle toward the bathroom, his desire for me to get my stuff and leave unspoken but clear. If I was still there when he came out in a robe, there would be a story about how he needed to make a conference call before bed, but if I wanted, he could try to call me next time I was in town.

As soon as I was gone, he'd sit there in that empty room, the smell of sex thick as he looked down at his hands, that were just starting to tremble again. He might take a few shots from the minibar before crawling into bed and turning off the light. And as the sound of the air conditioner filled the room, he would ask himself why he'd pushed me out the door so quickly. He would cradle the extra pillow and wish it was me as he drifted off into another sleepless night of misery.

The next morning it would start all over again.

I pushed away from the bar so quickly my stool fell out from under me. I crashed to the bar floor and my glass shattered next to me. The man, who was just an older me, reached down to offer me a hand. His face was full of concern and he spoke in a calm and empathic tone, but I couldn't hear anything over the blood rushing in my ears. My hands jerked away from him as he tried to help me up. I was pretty sure if we made contact with each other, one of would cease to exist.

The sad part was, I didn't know if I did or did not want it to be me who vanished.

This was who I'd become if I let Matt slip away. This old and battered man whose eyes held the same sadness I imagined in cows as they stumbled down the ramp in a slaughterhouse. It wasn't that they were sad about their impending doom; they were sad, and he was sad, because they and he had no idea how to stop their doom from swallowing them. I would end up in Foster, maybe grow addicted to online porn, maybe find random internet hookups with married and confused guys to fill the time. If I kept myself fit, I could coast off my looks well past fifty, but it wouldn't change the fact that I was a fifty-year-old man trolling the internet for love and or sex.

"Are you okay?" the other me asked as he pulled his hand away.

"No" was all I could spit out as I found my feet and backed away from him. I reached into my pocket and threw some bills at the bartender. "Keep it," I said as I turned and raced out of the airport bar. I forced myself to not look back at the other me.

Because I was pretty sure he wasn't going to be there.

I had reached the point where the paths diverged and had turned toward the one less taken. I was going to follow the one that led to Matt.

I was jogging to the front to grab a cab when I dialed his cell again. I heard the muffled sound of the cartoon mouse singing to the moon. I froze as Matt's phone went to voicemail and the singing stopped. I had teased Matt relentlessly about his choice of ringtones the first time I heard it. The ringtone was the movie version of "Somewhere Out There," not even the Linda Ronstadt version but the one actually sung by the mouse. I held my phone out and pushed redial.

Fievel began to sing again.

I moved toward it and heard the tail end of a conversation. "…idea what it is. All I know is that it won't shut up." There was a steward talking to an attendant, their luggage rolling behind them. The man was holding up Matt's phone in frustration. "This is what I get for being nice. I should have just left it on the fucking plane and…."

"I'll take it," I said, stepping in front of them and turning around.

They both paused and gave me a look. I could tell neither of them knew what I was talking about. Gesturing to the phone, I said, "I know whose phone that is. I'll take it."

The steward's face went from mild surprise to stark disbelief in half a second. "Oh right. What a coincidence," he said to his friend. They both started to move around me.

I pushed Redial again. Fievel began to sing about out there again.

"Seriously, that's me calling. I know whose phone that is," I said, holding my phone up. He still didn't believe me and answered it to make sure. "See? I'm not lying."

He sighed and hung up. "Fine. But tell your *friend* his fag hag is a fucking bitch." Without another word, he deposited the phone in my hand and walked away.

I held it tightly, knowing this was a sign from on high that I was on the right path.

MATT

HE WAS standing there. He was really fucking standing right there.

"I found your address under your settings," he said, still holding my phone out to me. "You know, in every romantic comedy, this is where you throw your arms around me and we kiss."

That broke me out of my stupor.

"This is not a movie," I snarled as I took my phone back. "And if it was, trust me, it would not be a romantic comedy." Though I wanted to do nothing more than slam the door in his face, there was no way I could bring myself to do it. He had flown all the way out here, and though my cell phone was not a glass slipper, in the twenty-first century it was a close equivalent. "Well, you might as well come in before my neighbors think we're haggling over the price of sex or something."

He quickly rushed inside before I could change my mind. "I can't believe you pay for sex, much less haggle over the price for it," he said as I slammed the door.

"Don't!" I said, turning to face him. "Do not come in here and be all charming and shit." The smile on his face vanished, and I tried to banish the image of an oversized puppy looking guilty after being caught peeing on the carpet. "I get it. I was stupid and we rushed things and it freaked you out. Fine. But do not come in here and start flirting with me all over again because I can't take it, Tyler. My heart just can't...." I took a gasping breath as I struggled to hold back tears. He edged toward me with his hands out as if he was going to catch me, but I held up one finger that froze him in his steps. "I am not in need of saving."

"Matt, I am so sorry...," he began to explain.

"I know! You're sorry, I'm sorry, who cares? This is where we are now." I looked at him as I fought the physical desire to touch him again. "If you came looking for forgiveness, Tyler, fine. You're absolved. Now go and sin no more."

He was silent for several seconds before uttering quietly, "I came here for you."

There was an actual pain in my chest as I felt my emotions begin to stew in anger. "Goddammit, stop!" I screamed. "Just stop trying to—" I fought to find the words and failed pretty badly. "—to do that thing you do. Stop being adorable, stop being hot, and stop looking at me like that. I can't handle this."

"Matt," he said in a careful tone, "I didn't just come here to apologize, which I do, by the way. Yes, I freaked, but that's on me, not you. I wasn't ready for any of that and I panicked. I tried to ignore it because I don't know how to deal with feelings like that." I gave him a wary look, and he added, "I'm serious! Every relationship I have ever had with a guy was some form of emotional chicken. They were just a series of endurance tests to see which of us would end up admitting they liked the other one first. In my entire life, I never had a guy just come out and say 'I like you' before."

"Well, now you have," I said, knowing I was pouting before the words even came out of my mouth.

He gave me those sad, sad eyes and asked, "We really can't get past this? I came all this way to get you."

I exploded. "You shouldn't have let me go in the first place!" It was a toss-up as far as which one of us was more startled by my outburst. I was betting on me. I forced myself to take a deep breath and try again. "I wanted you to tell me to stay when I was leaving. This isn't coming from a place of love, Tyler. This is you reacting to an ultimatum. I mean, who were we fooling? We didn't even date. We met in an electronics store and then spent the next week hiding in your bed. That's not much of a relationship."

I saw his eyes get wide as something passed through his mind. "You're right, so let's fix that. What are your plans for tomorrow night?"

That came out of left field. "Um, nothing. Why?"

My "nothing" seemed to stun him. "No seriously, what were your plans?"

"I don't have any," I said slowly, trying to impart to him the vast nothing that was my tomorrow night.

He ran a hand through his hair, a sure sign he was confused. "I thought that was why you left when you did."

"I left because I was tired of feeling like I was stalking you," I said as my voice got harsher.

"No, I got that," he said, sounding as if he was trying to figure out who killed Ms. Scarlet in the study. "So you really weren't going to do anything tomorrow night?"

"Oh, for fuck's sake! Why would I?" I exclaimed.

"Because it is New Year's Eve, dumbass," he answered, sarcasm coating every single syllable.

Now I felt stupid. "It is?"

He ignored my question. "Okay, so look, I screwed up. I should have said something in Foster, and that is on me. But I did come thousands of miles to chase you, so that should rate me at least one date, right?" I nodded slowly, not sure if I understood what he was saying. "So let me take you out for New Year's Eve. If at midnight you don't want to kiss me, I will respect that and head home the next day. But if you do kiss me, you admit there is something here between us."

"That isn't fair! You know I want to kiss you," I protested.

He gave me that damn grin, and I felt something melt deep inside me. "Well then, that makes my job pretty easy, right?"

"Forget it," I said, crossing my arms across my chest.

The grin faded fast. "Fine, you want to kiss me, but now you know it means more than a kiss. So go out with me tomorrow, and if you don't want to see me anymore, don't kiss me."

I still felt like I was being conned. "What if I just say I don't want to kiss you right now?"

"Then I would say you have nothing to lose by going out with me tomorrow, right?"

Damn, he was making sense.

"Okay, fine. But you are not sleeping here," I said quickly before I changed my mind on that. "This is a real first date, which means you have to jump through all the hoops."

"I will be all Michael Jordan up in this shit," he said eagerly.

"That means dinner and entertainment." He nodded quickly. "And when you make reservations, make them for four."

"Four?" he asked, looking like a cartoon coyote slamming into a wall. "Why four?"

"Because," I said, smiling. "One of the hoops is Sophia."

If this had been a movie, there would have been a crash of thunder and ominous organ music playing.

TYLER

I WENT to a local men's clothing store and spent as much money as I could afford on something to wear. There weren't many options left as far as things to do for New Year's Eve, but I was determined to find something special.

Something special for four people.

Matt had described Sophia in great detail in our time together, and I assure you I was not looking forward to this at all. Bad enough I didn't have a clue how to plan a date with a guy, but adding in his sarcastic "friend" and her date made the whole thing almost impossible.

The key word there was "almost."

That night, sitting in my hotel room browsing through the stack of brochures about local attractions I had found in the lobby, I struck gold. There was a nearby theater that served dinner and drinks during the movie, and for New Year's Eve they had a double feature—*Sixteen Candles* and *Pretty in Pink*. It took me almost fifteen minutes of begging to convince the guy on the other end that it was a matter of life and death that I got a table for what he was describing as a sold-out show. After an offer of my firstborn, which he knew was a sham, and triple the ticket cost, I had the very last table for the night.

What I'd accomplished seemed like a miracle. In one fell swoop, I'd covered dinner, entertainment, and even drinks. Also, I figured the movie would buy me some cover from Sophia, since all she could do was give me dirty looks instead of talking over dialogue. I knew, too, that if some guy had taken me on this date, he would have scored points.

Problem was, I needed more than a few points to tie this game up.

I tossed and turned all through the night. A strange bed coupled with the fact there was no way to know how tomorrow night was going to go gave me little sleep. Somewhere around ten, the phone woke me up from what must have been a nightmare the way I was sweating through the sheets. It took me a few tries to grab the phone before the receiver made it to my ear.

"Hullo?" I asked, burying my head under the pillow as I tried to escape the sun.

There was a slight pause. "Tyler?" Matt asked. "Are you still asleep?"

Forcing myself not to groan, I answered with a weak, "Kinda. What's up?"

"I just wanted to make sure everything was set for tonight." He was using his best "I am trying not to show any emotion in my words" voice, but I could hear the worry anyway.

"Yeah. I think you'll like it," I assured him. Silence followed for so long I thought we might have gotten disconnected. "Hello?"

"I'm here," he said quietly. "What are we doing?"

I sighed as I sat up. "I'm trying to make a bad thing better." I had no idea if the bad thing was what I had done or my life in general.

"And then what?" He was probably biting his nails down to nubs, which was something I had discovered he did when nervous.

"Then we figure out what we want to do?" I offered. "I really don't know, Matt. I just know I like you."

"We live thousands of miles apart," he countered.

"What happened to moving?" I teased. When he didn't comment, I knew it had been a bad idea. "I don't know what we do. I really don't. But can you tell me there isn't something here? That you don't feel it too? Because if you don't, just tell me."

"I thought I made my feelings pretty clear." His voice had gone cold.

"And now I'm trying to make mine as clear. I don't know what else to do." I swore to myself that I wasn't going to plead.

"I don't either," he answered after a few seconds.

"Just try to keep an open mind tonight," I asked him. "Try and give this a chance?"

"I'll try," he said, convincing neither of us.

"So, pick you guys up at around six?" I said, trying to change the subject.

"Sure. See you then."

I did not like the feeling of finality when he hung up the phone.

Instead of dwelling on things, I got up and turned on the shower. I was going to force this morning to get better even if it killed me.

I grabbed a quick breakfast and set out to find somewhere that could give me a trim before I had to be at Matt's. My first thought was to just find a barbershop nearby and get my usual done, but then inspiration hit me. I was in San Francisco, which meant there was an entire part of town that catered to the gay community. I hailed a cab and told the driver to take me to the Castro. I waited for him to say something in response, give me a look, anything out of the ordinary, but instead he just nodded and pulled out into traffic.

I had always pictured San Francisco as a much larger city than the one I was riding through now. I don't mean there wasn't a plethora of buildings and houses all around, but the streets just seemed so narrow they made the buildings on either side loom over us, making me feel even smaller. I couldn't tell if what we were stuck in counted as real traffic, or if it was just the lack of space, but it seemed like there were people everywhere. The city was cleaner than I imagined a city would be, not that I had this image of filth or anything. The streets and sidewalks were nothing like I had ever seen.

Our crawl across town took almost thirty minutes.

It occurred to me that, if I had had any idea where I was going, I could have walked faster than traffic was moving. Since I had time, I wondered why I hadn't walked. It wasn't as if I couldn't follow a map, and it couldn't have been that complicated a journey. We made another half block before the cabbie had to put on the brakes again, and I realized it hadn't even occurred to me to try to hoof it. The image of me—a huge countrified hick cowering in the back of a cab, scared that the big, bad city was going to get him—was embarrassing to a fault.

Or was I afraid of the Castro?

"Can you pull over here?" I told the driver.

"Here?" he asked, looking at me, confused. "This isn't Castro!" he said in halting English.

I handed him a twenty and got out. "I'm good," I said, waving. "Thanks."

When he saw I wasn't asking for change, he waved back and took off into traffic.

"Okay, hotshot," I said to myself as I pulled out my phone. "Put your money where your mouth is." I asked my phone for directions to the Castro. The computer voice was as nonjudgmental as the cabbie's had been, and she began to give walking directions.

I am not making something up or exaggerating when I say the buildings seemed to get brighter and more colorful the closer I got. Rainbow flags were displayed everywhere, making the whole block look as if it was a new attraction at Disneyland called Gayland. There were a few cafés with tables set up outside, and as I walked by, I saw pairs of men drinking coffee while they talked. A couple of them held hands across the table.

Almost every single one of them paused and watched me walk by.

I don't say that as a humble brag or anything. I say it because their staring made me way more uncomfortable than it should have. It wasn't as if they were all winking at me and drooling, but it was obvious that they paused and glanced as I got closer. I wasn't sure if they were cruising me or just wondering if I had gotten lost, but there was no way they weren't looking.

I began to get really self-conscious when I asked my phone for a barbershop nearby.

"You know, in the old days we just used our eyes," a deep, husky voice said from behind me. I turned and saw what had to be the world's biggest drag queen smoking outside a salon. I don't mean big as in fat, I mean big as in almost six feet five and wide as a linebacker. I openly stared and gaped. There was no way I could stop myself from the reaction.

He, she… okay, look, I have no idea what the protocol on these things is, but I was taught you should address people by the name they give you, even if you know their name is something else. James becomes Jimmy, Mikey preferred Michael, and some guys dressed as women. Which meant I should and would address her as a female even though I knew better. So you will excuse my pronoun choice.

She chuckled and shook her head at my reaction. "Take your time, sweetie. It's a lot to absorb."

My manners snapped back and I looked away sheepishly. "I'm sorry, that was uncalled for."

"No, being born a hairy lumberjack of a guy was uncalled for—what you just did was expected." She held out a huge paw of a hand that was adorned with a rather stunning set of ruby nails. "Patricia," she said as we shook. "And no, I was not a Pat before all of this. I just liked the name. So you're due for your thousand-mile checkup?"

I just stood there for a moment. "What?"

She laughed at my confusion. "Your hair, silly. Are you looking for a trim?" I nodded mutely, not trusting my mouth anymore. "Well, come on, then. You're going to start a riot standing out here on the sidewalk looking like that."

She ushered me in. "Looking like what?" I asked as she closed the door behind us.

"Looking like you play the bad boy with a heart of gold on a CW show, that's what. Have a seat," she said, gesturing to one of the leather stylists' chairs. The place was very obviously a high-scale kind of place to get a haircut. I had never ventured into one of these before; my mom or Gus down on First Street always took care of my hair needs in the past. I sat down and felt the chair ease me into it. Immediately, I swore silently that I needed a chair like this back home to watch college football over the weekend.

She handed me a glass of wine, which took me aback. I had never been offered alcohol during a haircut. "So I'm going to go out on a limb and say you aren't from here, right?" she asked me as we stared at each other in the mirror.

"I'm from Foster," I said, and then added a hasty, "Texas."

"Ah, the home of steers and queers," she observed before putting her glass down and running a hand over the top of my head. "I don't see no horns on you, boy." I didn't answer, and she added, "*Full Metal Jacket*?" I shook my head no, and she sighed. "I swear, finding a queer who likes a good war movie is impossible." She gestured at my hair. "So what are we doing with this?"

"Wait! You know I'm gay?" I asked, starting to turn around.

She spun me back to face the mirror. "You do know you're gay, right? Because, I'm going to be honest, I don't have the endurance for another confused closet case from a red state right now."

I made eye contact with her in the mirror. "You could really tell I'm gay?"

She rolled her eyes. "You can try to hide it with the short haircut, polo shirts, and khakis, but yeah, you were clocked. So just a trim or going for something adventurous today?"

My mind was like a dog chasing its own tail as I tried to comprehend what she was saying. "I really look gay?" I asked, more out loud than to her.

She gave me a sympathetic look as she nodded. "I hate to break it to you, but straight guys don't try this hard to look straight. It looks more like a Halloween costume than an actual outfit."

That was ironic coming from a man who was dressed in heels and what had to be the only triple-X silk blouse sold at Dillard's. "This is just how I dress," I explained.

"Oh God, this is what I get for opening my mouth," she said, walking over to the chair next to me and sitting down. Turning toward me, she crossed her legs and smiled at me, looking like a cross-dressing wrestler who had her own talk show. "Okay, let me guess. You live in a small town." Nod. "And no one knows you're gay except for a few friends, and even then it isn't public knowledge." Another nod. "You were a jock in high school and dated girls all the way to college." Slow nod. "You moved back for whatever reasons and are single and a little bit lonely. Am I right?" Shocked nod. "Right, so this," she said, gesturing to my clothes, "is not an outfit as much as it is camouflage, which is not saying you are just dying for a tight V-neck sweater and skinny jeans, but the thought of dressing any different just never crosses your mind, because if you did, you would have your third strike."

"Third?"

She began to count them off on her nails. "One, you're way too handsome to be single. Two, there isn't a straight guy who isn't from Utah that is as clean as you are, which means the third would be having a fashion sense. At that point, it's just a matter of months before someone adds one and one and one and gets queer."

Words refused to come to my mouth, much less leave it.

"So yeah, out here you look like you're a Mormon missionary who broke away from his handler or someone who is trying way too hard not to look gay. And the only people who try to do that *are* gay. See? Welcome to CSI: Fag. Now, your hair?"

It took me almost a minute to repeat, "But I've always dressed like this." There was no way it didn't sound like an excuse.

"I know, and when did that start? When you were trying to be the straightest man alive in high school, and then big jock on campus at college. Both times you were terrified of being found out." She got up and poured us each another glass of wine. "Look, how you dress is your business. I'm just answering your question. Yes, in this city, in this part of town, you look very gay. And not the good kind." She handed me my glass. "So, a little off the top or something more?"

I told her what I wanted and settled into silence as she put the smock over my chest. She began telling me all about the parties that were going on tonight, but my mind was nowhere near this room. Was I that obvious? Was I that predictable? Patricia here knew my whole life story without us ever speaking a word, which was as depressing as it was alarming. I had never thought of myself as a confused gay-guy stereotype, but hearing the words coming out of her mouth, it was hard to deny it.

And then it hit me.

"You were the same way," I said out loud, interrupting her. She stopped cutting and looked at me in the mirror. "You know all that because you were like me once."

She smiled at me. "Honey, in one way or another, everyone is like that at least once." She saw the look of determination on my face and nodded. "Yeah, I spent high school and a tour in the Marines trying my best to be the Brawny lumberjack guy they have on the paper towels. All big and strong, plaid-wearing alpha male, the last person in the world people would think liked dick."

"What happened?" I asked her, genuinely curious.

"I was miserable," she said with a little scoff. "The real me was dying inside, and if I didn't change, I was going to die. Maybe not physically and maybe not all at once, but in more ways than one, I was going to die. So I gave it all up. I just walked away from my life and tried to find the me I wanted to be."

"And that you dresses up as a woman?"

Her voice got harsh. "I'm not dressed this way because I suffer from a rare form of gay Tourette's that causes me to break out in Celine Dion and want to be dressed right just in case. This is what makes me happy, way more happy than I was, pretending to be like you."

"I'm sorry. I wasn't trying to imply anything," I said quickly.

"Yes, you were," she said, pushing my chin at my chest. "And it's okay. Most people assume I'm dressed as a woman, you know, like I'm in drag. I am not a female impersonator, and this is not drag. This is who I am. There is a difference. We are all somebody inside, and most of the time we are too chickenshit to stare that person in the face. I stared into the abyss, and when it stared back, it was wearing Revlon photo-ready concealer and cherry blossom lipstick."

It made me wonder who I was inside and if I could stare him in the face.

"And presto," she said, turning me back toward the mirror. "One well-groomed, yet still masculine, trim with no frills." I looked in the mirror and was impressed. She did great work. "You sure I can't talk you into frosted tips? You'd be beating them off with a stick."

I laughed nervously and shook my head. "I think I'm good."

She laughed with me. "I know you're good. I was just trying to help you out."

I got up and made my way to the register and pulled out my wallet. "You do good work," I told her, handing her way too much money. When she took it, I held on to it and she made eye contact. "And the haircut was good too."

"You're welcome," she said, smiling. She rang up the cut. "You need a cab? Because trust me, if you keep walking around here looking like that, someone is going to cruise you. Hard."

I looked outside and thought about it. "You know what?" I said, grinning. "I think that's okay."

MATT

"ARE YOU serious?"

Forcing back a sigh, I leaned my head into my shoulder to hold the phone in place while I pulled off my pants. "You were the one who wanted to meet him."

Sophia's laugh was not pleasant. "Yeah, I wanted to meet him so I could kick him in the balls for treating you like shit. Not to waste my New Year's Eve with him."

"He didn't treat me like shit. He just freaked out because we moved too fast," I reminded her as I sat down on my bed and started to pull my socks off. "He flew thousands of miles to make it up to me."

"Oh God! Are you really going to sit there and make excuses for him? You sound like a battered housewife. 'He only hits me when I make him mad.' Come on, Matt!"

There was no way to prevent the sigh escaping my mouth this time.

"And don't give me that sigh. That is your 'You don't know what you're talking about, Sophia' sigh, and in this case, I do know what I'm talking about. You dating another asshole."

"We aren't dating, and he isn't an asshole," I protested, but it was a mistake.

"You can't be this desperate, Matt. Honestly, you can't just settle for the first guy who wanders along and...."

That was a step too far.

"Okay, look. I am not desperate, and this is not a battered-wife thing. He asked me out and that's that. If you can't go and be civil, then tell me now and I'll tell him it's just the two of us."

The silence between us was deafening because neither one of us even breathed.

"I'm just trying to help you, Matt. Of course I'll go tonight," she said after what seemed like a year of not talking.

The problem was, I knew she was lying. I knew she was just waiting to get Tyler in a room so she could give him a piece of her mind. And even though I knew what she was planning, I said nothing because I suppose part of me wanted her to do it as well. The part of me that liked Tyler too much, the part of me from high school that still thought he walked on water, the part that refused, even now, to believe he was gay. The part of me that had always been content to just sit in the corner and let other people do the dirty work made me say, "Okay, I'll give you a call once I know what's going on."

I hung up the phone knowing I had just made a huge mistake.

What does it say about me that I knew exactly what I had done wrong, but instead of fixing it, I just sat there and waited for time to pass? Worse, how many other times had I done this and never noticed? My dad's words came echoing back, that if I'd moved from Foster to be happy but was still miserable, then maybe Foster was never the problem. I did want to be happy. I really did.

After a while, I wasn't sure if I was saying it because it was true or because I wanted it to be true.

I got into the shower and began to get ready, knowing it would distract my thoughts long enough for them to grow quiet again. Drying my hair, I walked out, saw the suit I had laid out on the bed, and froze. It looked like one of my father's suits to me, and that was distressing for some reason. I did the math and realized that by my age, my dad had served in the military, married my mom, and had two kids, with a third on the way. His life was well into the middle part and mine was nowhere. Was this how I was going to be? Endlessly stuck in neutral until my life started? What was I waiting for? What exactly did I think the starting pistol sounded like?

A knocking at my door broke me out of my stupor.

Without thinking, I opened the door and found Tyler holding a bouquet of flowers in his hands. From the look of shock on his face, I had missed something. Like getting dressed. "Um, come in," I said, retreating to my room, hoping the towel around my waist covered enough.

He closed the door and called after me, "Don't hurry on my account." I could hear the smile in his voice from my room.

I pulled my clothes on in a rush, frustrated with myself that I had lost so much time in the mental masturbation that was my life. I checked myself in the mirror, hated what I saw, and walked out of my room. I hated the way my breath paused a second as I saw him looking through my bookshelf while he waited. He turned and smiled at me, and I felt everything inside me go to mush.

Forcing the feeling away, I asked him, "So do I get to know what our plans are yet, or is it still a surprise?"

"Still a surprise," he said, picking the flowers off the coffee table. Walking over, he handed me the flowers. "These are for you."

Refusing to let my emotions get the better of me, I took them and headed to the kitchen to put them in water. "Thanks" was my only reply.

"You know, we don't have to do this," he said as I filled a vase with water. "I can just go if you aren't interested in the date."

Lack of interest wasn't the problem at all—in fact, just the opposite. It was the knee-jerk feeling that this man was perfect that had led me to this point in the first place. My attraction was as persistent as a dog that keeps trying to jump on someone even though its owner is screaming at it to get down. "I'm fine," I said neutrally. "I'm up for it if you are."

He cocked his head and paused, as if he could read the feelings behind my words. For a moment, I thought he was going to call me out on my bullshit, but instead he just shrugged and asked, "Okay. Are we waiting for your friend or we picking her up?"

As if on cue, my door burst open and Sophia spilled into my apartment. "I'll get you, my pretty....," she screeched and then stopped when she saw I wasn't alone. "Oh" was all she said, mentally and physically checking herself. What's-his-name walked in behind her. I could see in the way she lost her momentum that Sophia thought Tyler was hot but there was no way she was going to admit it. "You must be the boy who broke Matt's heart," she said, walking across the room to him, her hand extended as if she expected him to kiss her ring.

She stopped in midstep when he smiled at her and said, "You must be the fag hag."

I thought she was going to explode as she glared at him in silence. Instead, she moved past him and hugged me. "Happy New Year, Matty!" As she squeezed me, she whispered. "I hate him."

And the night had just begun.

TYLER

I HONESTLY had been on some bad dates before, but so far, this one was taking the cake.

Sophia stopped attacking me directly, instead opting for the always fun passive-aggressive approach. When we got to my rental car, she made some underhanded comment about it. I didn't catch the exact sentence, but I heard the word "cheap" and that was enough. Her boyfriend creeped me out because he kept staring at me like I was a piece of prime rib and he was a starving wolf. If he wasn't gay, then he was living in a walk-in closet that had to have its own en suite.

Matt looked more and more miserable the longer we drove through the crowded San Francisco streets. I would have never guessed the city would be this claustrophobic from what I had seen on TV and in the movies, but trying to drive made me feel like Godzilla. We got stuck at an intersection, which gave Sophia the opportunity to pounce. "So where exactly are we going?" she asked, leaning forward from the back seat.

"It's kind of a surprise," I told her, trying to find a way to shove her back without being rude.

"Well, I hate surprises," she said, not moving an inch.

I mentally tried to will the light to change as I forced myself to stay calm. "Well, the surprise isn't for you, so I think you're safe." She refused to budge and glared at me in the rearview mirror. She was so busy giving me the stink eye she didn't see the light change. I did, and I shoved the accelerator down in an attempt to get through the intersection before the light changed again.

Sophia gave a small yelp as she tumbled back into her seat. I saw Matt cover his mouth to hide his laughter while we followed the flow of traffic. Sophia went back to silent seething that lasted all the way to the theater. We pulled into the parking lot, and I heard her go off again. "Really? A couple of movies that we could have watched on Netflix? *This* is your big surprise?"

I found us a parking space and began counting to myself in my head as a way of ignoring her diatribe. After I turned off the car, I turned to Matt. "Do you remember when the Vine had these playing, and Eli Cole and his friends ended up setting that smoke bomb off and everyone ran out?" Matt nodded with a small grin on his face. "Well, I never told anyone this, but I was with them that night, so it was kind of my fault too. So I thought I owed you a repeat showing."

His face lit up, and his grin turned into a huge smile. I thought for a second we were going to kiss, but Sophia ruined that as she burst out from the back seat. "Oh, nice. You were a douche in high school and it's taken you this long to make up for it?"

"I think it's romantic," her date said to me. He sounded again like he was hitting on me.

"Shut up!" she said, jamming her arm into his side. "I hope they serve drinks," she added, getting out of the car. The guy with her slowly followed her, his eyes still on me, his lips still turned up in that creepy smile.

"So he is…?" I started to ask Matt about Sophia's date.

He nodded. "Oh yeah, completely." He took my hand and squeezed it. "This is an awesome idea! I'm glad I came."

"So am I." I began to lean forward. I saw him move toward me before I closed my eyes.

"*Come on!*" Sophia roared, banging on Matt's window. "It's freezing out here."

The moment was sufficiently ruined, so we got out of the car and raced into the theater. Once inside, we were seated at a table, and a waiter took our drink orders while we looked over the menu. I wasn't sure if alcohol was going to help or hinder the night, but by the time the first drinks arrived, I knew it couldn't get much worse.

Halfway through her second margarita, Sophia stared intensely at me from across the table. "So you were what? A total closet case in high school and college?"

She of course had asked in the middle of me taking a drink, so it was all I could do to not sputter out an answer. Before I could speak, Matt chimed in with, "I never said that, and you know as well as I do that I was in the closet for high school and most of college too."

The facts rolled off Sophia's back like water off a duck. "Sweetie, you're still in the closet," she said, looking back to me. "You were, right?"

Putting my drink down, I said, "There are a lot of people who are confused about their sexuality at all ages." I looked over to her "boyfriend" and then back at her. "We all get there in our own time."

Obviously not the answer she had been looking for. "Right, but you dated girls? And never told them you liked dick."

"Um, I dated girls too," Matt added, but she ignored him altogether, instead focusing on me.

"These girls had no idea you were gay, and you dated them?" she asked again.

"Yeah," I admitted. "I did do that."

"Kind of a shitty thing to do, don't you think?" She leaned forward with the same intensity I had seen Barbara Walters give in interviewing mob bosses.

There were several different ways I could have answered that, but I opted for the one she probably wasn't expecting. "Yeah, it was shitty. In fact, one of the things I most regret about growing up was lying to people about who I was. I felt like shit every time I led a girl on, which is one of the many reasons I just sat down and accepted I was gay instead of trying to continue lying."

You could see by the look in her eyes these were not the words she expected to come out of my mouth. In fact, from the way Matt was looking at me, they were not the words anyone was expecting.

"I didn't know you hated it that much," Matt told me.

I shrugged and took another drink. "You didn't ask." I wished I didn't sound as bitter as I did, but I couldn't help it. There was so much ground Matt and I hadn't covered over Christmas that it seemed impossible for either of us to know anything about each other. I wondered again why I was here and trying so hard.

"Yeah, right," Sophia said after a few seconds of uncomfortable silence. "You just felt like crap every time you nailed a girl. Like there was a gun to your head."

"It wasn't a gun," I answered as calmly as I could muster. "It was something much worse I was afraid of."

I could see her opening her mouth to ask what could be worse than a gun to my head when Matt answered. "Having people find out you were gay and treating you different. I think getting shot would have been better than having to go to school with everyone knowing I was gay."

"Oh please," Sophia said as the lights began to dim for the movie. "Plenty of people out there are gay, and they are just fine."

I lowered my voice, but it was hard since I felt like screaming at her. "It isn't that easy in a place like Foster," I hissed at her. "Especially if you play sports."

She didn't even look at me, instead waving me off with one hand. "Closet cases always have an excuse."

Now I wanted to jump across the table and throttle her, no matter how much I hated guys who put their hands on women. I looked over at Matt, who gave me a small, apologizing smile. "Wasn't making an excuse, was answering your question."

She just looked over at me with a condescending smile and said, "Your movie's starting."

I looked at the candle-filled jar that made the table's centerpiece and wondered if I could crack her across the skull with it.

They started with *Pretty in Pink*, a move that did not go well with Sophia because she sighed and muttered. "Awesome, two hours about a perfectly fine girl who ends up choosing the douchebag in the end." She looked across to me. "I have seen this story way too much lately."

Matt threw his napkin at her. "Knock it off," he grumbled. She settled down some as the movie began.

We got to the computer lab scene when they brought us our first dish. The menu had a variety of items from burgers all the way to Italian food. It wasn't fancy, but I had never eaten dinner in a movie theater before, so it was all new to me. I'm sure no one is surprised to hear Sophia did not like her meal at all.

"Well, you can really see where the sixteen bucks went in this dish," she said, pushing the plate back. "It's like being in a Gordon Ramsay show while they play John Hughes."

Her boyfriend said with his mouth full, "I kinda like it."

She batted at his arm. "No, you don't."

He paused, a noodle halfway out of his mouth. "I don't?" She shook her head no. The end of the noodle slipped into his mouth as he looked down at his plate sadly.

"It's not bad," Matt said, taking a bite of his burger.

"Which is a way of saying it's not good," she countered.

I had already lost my temper a while back; now it was just a battle to keep my tongue in check. A task that I was failing at badly. "Then order something else," I said to her.

She turned back to the movie. "No use. Not sure what I was expecting, ordering food in a place with sticky floors."

We sat in relative silence for the rest of the movie. Matt and I picked at our food, too upset to really enjoy it, and the other guy just looked down at his plate from time to time like a kid who was being punished. The lights came up as the credits rolled, and a good number of people got up to stretch or use the bathroom or even go outside and smoke.

Sophia took it as her cue for round two.

"So explain to me why we aren't somewhere fun, like a club. A gay club," she added for emphasis. "Like normal gay guys do."

"Normal?" I asked with skepticism in my voice. "So normal gay guys who are lonely go to clubs to celebrate?"

"They do in my world," she said, finishing her glass of wine. "The only ones who don't have issues with being gay."

"I don't have issues with being gay. I've been to plenty of gay clubs before. I just don't find they are the best place for a date." My voice was rising with anger, but I was way past caring.

"And bringing another couple is a good choice?" she asked me.

"That was my choice," Matt interjected.

She ignored him. "I just think you don't want the competition a gay bar brings."

I laughed out loud before I could stop myself. "Competition? You think I brought him here because I think someone better-looking is going to hit on Matt?"

"Someone who doesn't have issues with being gay."

I leaned forward "I don't have issues with being fucking gay."

"Prove it," she said with a smile.

Forty-five minutes later, we were walking to a gay bar.

MATT

As we filed into Strut, I kept yelling at myself to turn this date around and leave.

Sophia had been nonstop on Tyler the whole night, and I couldn't get her to let up. I admit I wasn't trying all that hard because I know talking to her is a wasted effort most of the time, but her goading him to take us here was a mistake. I'll try to explain.

There are gay bars. And there are *gay* bars.

Meaning there were bars gay guys went to and hung out in, and then there were bars that had an attitude. I'm not sure what your personal level of interaction with gay bars has been, but believe me when I say if you've been to one of the places with attitude, you know from your first step inside. Everyone is pretty, well-dressed, young, and likes to show off. What few clothes they are wearing are stylish, and of course let's not forget the very best in designer drugs. Places like Strut make things like Ecstasy not just popular but somehow glamorous to others. I wasn't a fan of Strut and others like it, but Sophia loved them and had always assured me if I was going to find someone, it would be in a place like this.

We paid the cover and walked in and were assaulted by a thundering backbeat from the music.

Tyler screamed something at me, but there was no chance of me hearing him. We followed Sophia and What's-his-name upstairs, where there were tables available. The music became a little muddled up here, making some forms of conversation possible. Tyler offered to grab us some drinks, and I took the moment to pull Sophia aside.

"What the hell are you doing?" I asked her over the music.

"I'm just looking out for you," she screamed back.

"You're attacking him." She nodded with a smile. "Why?"

"To see if he really is into you," she answered, which just made me more confused. "If he's willing to put up with me, then you know he's serious about being here for you. It's like a test."

I hated to admit it, but she was making some sense.

"You spent the last weeks chasing him—let him chase you for a while." I shouldn't have believed her, but I did. Tyler came back and put our drinks down before sitting next to me.

"So is this better?" he asked her across the table. She just shrugged and said something to What's-his-name. Tyler turned to me and asked, "Did you want to come here?"

I wasn't sure how to answer that, since we would have most likely have ended up here if he hadn't shown up, but *want* was a little too strong a word for my desire to be here. This was just what Sophia and most guys around here did. We went to Strut, we drank, we danced, and we pretended not to be that interested in any one guy. This was the gay life I had grown to know. It wasn't about like or dislike; it just was.

"Do you like it?" I asked him, curious what his answer would be.

He didn't even think about it. He just said "No" and took a sip of his beer. His eyes scanned the room in the same manner I had seen cops size up a room as they walked in the door. He was distrustful, almost hostile. In other words, he was everything I had been when I first arrived in the city.

"It's a fun place once you get used to it," I tried to tell him.

His gaze moved to me, and I swore it was as if he was staring through me. I could almost hear him flip through the possible responses to my statement; instead he gave me a small smile and nodded. "I bet."

This was miserable.

No one talked. We sat there, nursed our drinks, and watched the chaos move around us. The upstairs was basically a pit stop for the club, a place where you could drag the guy you met on the dance floor to so you could talk or just make out. More than a few couples were opting for the last choice, and it was hard not to stare.

I was about to turn to Tyler to say we could leave if he wanted to when someone tapped me on the shoulder.

It was Coffee Shop Boy.

Now, I name him that for a couple of reasons. One, because no matter how many times I had gone to the coffee shop and noted he was cute, I had never once caught his name. Hence the Coffee Shop. The last word is the important one, though. Boy. This guy was in no way a man yet. I mean, it wasn't like I was the old man of the mountain or anything, but he wasn't a day over twenty-two, which meant he was still smack in the middle of his "I have no idea who I am and could honestly give a fuck" phase—that space of time in the early twenties all gay men go through where they become a complete mess and then vow never to return to once they've outgrown it. Some guys phased out of it fast; others were well into their forties and still stuck in the middle of it.

I honestly hadn't realized I was past it until I looked up at him and realized he was not an actual person to me but in fact just Coffee Shop Boy.

It seemed a million years ago I had hit my head on the table because I was so flustered by his presence. Now he was just one more can of gasoline on the bonfire that was tonight. I smiled automatically but wasn't sure if I should stand up. To be honest, my first reaction was to yell "Go away!" at him, but since he had done nothing to warrant that, I just smiled and shook his hand. "Hey, you," I said lamely.

"Never seen you here before," he said, taking the one empty seat left at our table. He looked over at Sophia. "Hey, girl, what's up?"

They gave each other air kisses on the cheeks, and I knew this wasn't a disaster—this was a setup.

I turned back to Tyler, who was watching the exchange with the same look cops have when trouble walks into a room they're patrolling. "He works at the coffee shop we go to," I explained, trying to minimize his importance.

Coffee Shop Boy was faster than I gave him credit, though. "Hi, I'm Cody," he said, reaching across me and extending his hand to Tyler.

Tyler gave the boy a smile that didn't reach all the way up to his eyes and shook the hand. "Of course you are."

I'm pretty sure Coffee Sho—Cody couldn't hear across the table, 'cause he just smiled and nodded before looking to me. "So, funny seeing you here," he exclaimed, overjoyed.

I glanced at Sophia before nodding. "Yeah, it's random."

He looked around the bar for a moment, reminding me of a dog that had stuck its head out a car window for the first time. I wanted to try to explain to Tyler who this guy was, or better yet who he wasn't, when the boy, er, I mean Cody, looked back at me. "Hey, you want a drink?" I held my beer up, showing him I already had one. He didn't quite understand the gesture, because he nodded and stood up quickly. "Got it." Looking to the table, he asked, "You guys want anything?"

Sophia held up her drink, and he bopped off to the bar with a smile.

Turning back to Tyler, I tried to explain quickly. "He's a kid that works where we get coffee. I have no idea what he's doing here, and I swear to you it wasn't planned."

He wasn't looking at me, though. He was looking at Sophia.

She looked back over at him and gave him the same smile the Cheshire cat would give if he were a few pounds overweight and had learned to put his makeup on from drag queens. "Problem?"

Tyler put his beer down and said to me, "I need to use the head," and got up abruptly. What's-his-name got up at the same time, saying he needed to as well. They walked off, leaving Sophia and me alone.

"What did you do?" I said as soon as I was sure they were gone.

She leaned toward me so I could hear her better. "I just wanted to show you that he was not the only game in town. There are plenty of guys who would date you, Matt!"

I pointed to where Coffee Shop Boy was buying our drinks. "*That*? You want me to date that?"

"He's hot," she commented.

"He's a zygote," I countered. "I'm probably ten years older than him. What in the world could we talk about?"

She gave me a look, making it pretty clear we both knew I was closer to twenty years older, but she didn't say it out loud. Instead she said. "If you're with that boy and you're talking, trust me, Matt, you're doing it wrong." She sounded like some lame *Sex and the City* wannabe, and I lost it. I just lost it.

I pounded my hands on the table, making the bottles jump. "This isn't a fucking game," I screamed. "This is my life."

"You don't have a life," she shot back. "You have a job, a gym membership, and me. The closest thing you have to a relationship is with your phone, and it is sad. I'm trying to help you here."

I could see it in her face; she really thought she was helping. This wasn't spite or some weird way of her trying to inflict harm on me. She honestly thought she was doing me a favor. Which just made it all that much worse. "Do you even know me?" I asked her. "Do you even know who I really am? What I dream of? What I truly desire? Am I a person to you or just some gay guy you hang out with because you think gay guys are fun?"

She sputtered a response, but I could tell she had nothing of value to say. "I don't want this," I said, gesturing around us. "I don't like places like this. *You* do. I hate clubs. I hate cruising. I hate casual sex, and I hate that you think I'm some backward hick for thinking like that. There isn't a guidebook on how to be gay, and if there was one, it wouldn't be written by a fag hag!"

She looked like she had been slapped.

"Hey, did I miss anything?" Coffee Shop Boy asked, coming back with our drinks.

I spun and looked at him. "Did she call you and tell you to show up here tonight? Did she tell you I was interested in you or something?" He looked down instantly, and that was enough answer for me. "Sophia, this is hands down the worst thing you have ever done."

Which was when Tyler came back to the table and grabbed his coat. "I'm done," he said, pulling it on. "You are free to stay here and dance and flirt and do whatever you want," he said angrily. "But I'm done for tonight."

"I just wanted to meet you," Coffee Shop Boy said to me, seemingly unaware of Tyler's words.

"What happened?" I asked as my head began to pound from sensory overload.

"Let me guess?" Sophia interrupted. "You went to the bathroom and saw something your Midwest upbringing didn't allow? It's okay for you to sneak around and pretend to be straight for all those years, but what these guys do in a gay bar is too much?"

Tyler looked over at her, and I swore he was going to hit her. "You know what, lady? You are a complete bitch. I know I screwed up, and I flew thousands of miles to make things right. Matt has every right to be mad at me, but you? You I haven't done shit to."

"You hurt him. That was enough," she responded.

"If I was out to hurt him…," he began to answer and then trailed off. "Forget it."

Sophia stood up. She was pissed. "No, go for it. Hit me with your best shot. You have nothing on me."

Instead of taking the bait, he looked to me. "I'm going. I'm sorry for making you feel the way I did. You're a great guy, Matt. I hope you find what you're looking for."

Coffee Shop Boy looked confused. "Wait, so you were dating someone but just broke up with them?"

Sophia was not going to let it go. "No, come on. You're leaving, so tell me your big revelation. Show me how you aren't out to hurt Matt."

Which was when What's-his-name came running up to the table, breathless. "I wasn't propositioning him! It was a joke," he explained quickly.

Everyone turned to look at him.

Tyler gestured toward him and said to Sophia. "If I was an asshole, I would have taken your boyfriend up on the blowjob he offered me in the bathroom."

She looked at What's-his-name with her hands covering her mouth. She was beyond shocked, and all he could say was "It was a joke"?

She began swatting at him. "You said you weren't gay! You said you were over it!"

"Wait, you guys didn't know that guy was gay?" Coffee Shop Boy asked. "He's always making passes at me." Which just caused Sophia to start beating her now ex-boyfriend harder.

I turned back to Tyler to tell him this was not in any way what I wanted, that this entire thing had been a series of missed chances, and I didn't care anymore.

I wanted to say all that, but he was gone.

He was gone and the night was over.

TYLER

I WENT back to my hotel room and threw everything I had bought into bags and dropped my rental car off at the airport. I sat in the terminal until the night sky began to lighten with the hint of the coming day. As soon as the terminal opened, I pulled out my credit card and did something I had not done since I was seven years old and had the wind knocked out of me during Pop Warner practice and couldn't take a full breath for over ten minutes.

I bought a ticket to Florida and ran home to my mommy.

Brad had been given instructions to just shut the store down after New Year's, which meant I was in no hurry to get back to Foster. In fact, I knew there was nothing for me back in Foster at all.

That was far scarier than I wished to admit.

My parents were super supportive, but they knew something was wrong. Your adult son doesn't show up on your doorstep out of nowhere for a skinned knee. But instead of grilling me, they just kept their distance and let me decompress on my own. Common sense told me that if the first time you go out with a guy ends in disaster, there could be a number of reasons. By the second, and then the third, you began to wonder.

At my age, the only common factor left was me.

Maybe I just wanted to be single. Maybe deep down I never wanted to be in a relationship, so I went out of my way to sabotage myself when I was in one. Maybe I was just one of those people who were destined to be alone. Maybe it was all part of God's plan.

And maybe if I kept repeating all of the maybes, I would believe myself.

My mom made up the spare room without one question, which led me to believe Matt's mom had been talking to her. My dad started telling me about the local football while I looked around their living room. There was a wall of pictures of me, from baby pictures to a photo of me in my college uniform. I had seen these pictures my entire life, but I really looked at them now.

I was smiling in each one, and in each one it was a lie.

Most had a girl next to me who had no idea who she was standing next to. The wall of pictures was a monument to a lie that had consumed my early life. I thought about what Patricia had told me about my straight disguise and could see what she'd been talking about. I was basically wearing the same outfit I went to the Spring Formal in when I was fifteen. The only thing that had changed was I could admit I was gay when I was backed into a corner.

"You okay?" my dad asked, coming up next to me.

I shook my head no, though I couldn't explain myself.

I spent the first few days sitting in their backyard, watching the ocean play tag with little kids who populated the beach with their tourist parents. Their laughter sounded fake to me, which confused me until I realized it was because they were genuinely happy. There were no conditions on their glee, no restrictions on what they allowed to make themselves feel joy. They were happy because they wanted to be happy.

I wondered if that was true for being miserable as well.

Finally, after a week, my dad sat down next to me. He offered me a beer, which was his silent way of informing me we were about to have a conversation whether I liked it or not. I opened it and took a long drink, since I was pretty sure this was going to be like a root canal and this beer was the only Novocain I was going to get.

"Did I ever tell you what I was going to college for when I met your mom?"

I opened my mouth to answer and then paused. I had heard the story about how they met in college at a mixer and hit it off famously. She ended up getting pregnant with me, and she dropped out while he finished the semester before they both moved back to Foster. I knew that story well, but who my dad was before he met my mom was a mystery. I was just getting comfortable with the fact my parents were people outside of being my mom and dad. The thought that they might have wanted to be other things than my parents and owners of a sporting goods store kind of blew my mind.

"I was going to be an architect," he said wistfully, looking out across the water.

As soon as he said it out loud, it made perfect sense to me. My dad's whole life was about math and logic, which was why when I came out, he kind of had a short circuit for a while. On paper, I was a perfect straight jock. I was handsome, athletic, hardworking, not effeminate, and the girls liked me. In his mind, my life was locked in. I would be straight, married, and have kids by twenty-five. The world was like that to him, all math and numbers, which would make perfect sense to an architect.

"I was so sure I was going to go on and design bridges and skyscrapers," he said between sips. "I had my whole life planned out. Live in the city, have one of those bachelor apartments with a bar and a balcony. I would be the young-but-intelligent mastermind who would take the city by storm. I already had the pose I would use on my first magazine cover." He looked at me and put his hand on his chin with a seriousness that made me smile.

"So what happened?" I asked, thinking I knew the answer.

He looked over at me. "I met your mother and my life started over again." I felt my heart stop for a moment as I saw the love in his eyes. "Once she entered my life, I realized that all those plans were meaningless because they didn't include her. That's what love does, Tyler. It makes you realize how meaningless life can be alone. It just walks in and reorganizes everything the way it wants, and you sit there wondering how you ever got along before." He stared me right in the eyes, and his voice grew serious. "If you think doing something for love is too embarrassing or too demanding, then it isn't love. Love has no ego, it has no limits, and it should never make you feel smaller. If this thing with the Wallace boy made you feel like that, then it wasn't real. You have to believe that."

My eyes began to sting as I realized that was what I had done to Matt.

"I don't care if you like men or women." He paused. "Well, okay, I don't care now. All I want is for you to be happy, and I honestly don't know what to do to help you." He looked at me with such sympathy, with such sorrow, that it took a second for me to realize he felt sorry for me. "What can I do to make you happier, Tyler?"

For the first time since I arrived, I began to cry for my loss. And for the second time in my life, my father held me and told me it was going to be okay. The first being when I busted my knee in college and was told I would never play ball again. I felt tired. I felt drained....

I felt defeated. I felt lost.

MATT

TWO DAYS passed before I heard from Sophia again.

I should mention that I hadn't tried to contact her at all. I had been too busy trying to get Tyler on the phone. I was pretty sure the only way this entire experience could have ended up worse was if I had killed his dog or if I left a severed horse head in his bed. My first impulse was to apologize, but after a couple of days passed, I realized there wasn't much more to say.

Which was when Sophia ended up knocking on my door.

I opened it, and she gave me a huge smile that did nothing but make her look like a reptile exposing its teeth. "So where are we going tonight?"

Only eighteen years of my mother's upbringing prevented me from slamming the door in her face, and even then, it was a close call. "What do you want?" I asked her, imagining my breath fogging from the ice in my voice.

She paused. "What's wrong with you?" She tried to move past me, but I refused to budge. "Matt. What is wrong?"

My mind boggled that she had no idea. "Are you fucking kidding me?" I almost screamed at her. "You ruined my date." Which really meant "You ruined my life."

She rolled her eyes. "That jerk? Please." She looked at the arm that was still barring her entrance. "Are you going to let me in or just pout at me in the doorway?"

"Are you really clueless as to how mad I am?" I asked her, not moving my arm.

"About the asshole who walked out on you during New Year's Eve? You're mad at me for that?" She genuinely sounded surprised.

"You attacked him the entire night!" Now I *was* screaming.

"Because he was a dick. And I'm pretty sure he proved that by leaving."

"He left because your boyfriend tried to suck his dick in the bathroom."

She rolled her eyes again. "He offered. He didn't try to or anything. Besides, that's over. So let's go get messed up and complain about our love lives while we cruise boys."

It took me a second to realize she was not being sarcastic or ironic—she was really saying we should go do that for fun. Then I realized it was what I had been doing since I moved here, and up to now, all it had done was make me miserable. My mind began showing me night after night, like a flip-book of my entire life. It was just us going out every night we could, getting drunk, hitting on the wrong men, and then being miserable about it. Suddenly the older guys who looked like they had died on their barstools that populated every club made sense. These weren't losers or desperate people.

They were me in ten years.

People say the definition of insanity is doing the same thing over and over and expecting different results. If that was true, then being single and gay was the craziest thing in the world. This hadn't made me happy, wasn't making me happy, and sure in the hell was never going to make me happy. I had been so sure Foster was my problem and once I was beyond the city limits, I would somehow magically find happy. Maybe it was just a Midwest thing, but the Dorothy complex seemed to dominate the way I thought life would be.

I would leave on a tornado of my making and find myself in a magical land of color and song, where finding happiness would be as easy as following a brick road to a place where a faceless stranger would grant all my wishes. Of course, at the end of the story the hick realizes she just wants to go home.

"Are you even upset that you may have just run the best guy I've ever met out of town?"

It was a stupid question, but I had to hear the words come out of her mouth. "Me?" she asked, placing a hand on her chest. "No, that wasn't just a me-thing. We both did that. You wanted to tell him to go to hell, but as usual, Little Matty Wallace didn't have the balls so he needed big, bad Sophia to do it for him." She glared at me. "So before you start blaming people, you better make sure it's a table for two."

"Are you even upset for me?"

She laughed. "I don't see you broken up that my boyfriend turned out to be gay."

"*You knew that*!" I screamed at her. "Everyone in the world told you that, and still you ignored it. You'd have to be insanely stupid, or some part of you wanted this to happen just so you could be...." My words trailed off as the final shoe dropped in my mind.

"What, Matt?" she demanded. "Please dazzle me with your Midwest brilliance. I am on the edge of my seat."

"You want to be miserable," I said more than asking. "You like feeling like this."

She rolled her eyes and began to study her nails. "I don't like this feeling, sweetheart. This is just what life is. We date horrible men, they break our hearts, we go out, drink to forget them, and find new boys to replace them." She looked up at me, and I could tell she was deadly serious. "What exactly did you think dating was all about, Matt? This is what we do."

"Not anymore," I said, closing the door in her face.

TYLER

MY FATHER had a saying that had always unnerved me.

He used to say, "No matter how bad your life may get, I can walk out on the streets and find three people who have it worse in seconds." Being an only child, I had never believed him, because it had always been all about me, but I had never been able to debunk his theory. The saying had stuck with me, and I never forgot it.

I sat on the couch, feeling sorry for myself, when life took the opportunity to remind me that no matter how bad things were for me, someone had it worse.

My phone rang. I barely glanced at it since it was most likely Matt again. He had left a trail of voicemails but I hadn't even bothered. What was there to say? We were both sorry things crashed and burned and life sucks. The end. Except when I glanced over, I saw it wasn't Matt's number.

It was Brad.

I hadn't talked to him since I took off before New Year's. He had texted me and let me know the shop was locked up tight and all was good, and I had texted him back a thank-you. I knew if I called him, he would ask how things were going, and I did not want to break down and cry in front of a teenager. I assumed him calling meant something was up.

"What's going on, Brad?"

There was a pause, and I felt my entire body tense up. "Mr. Parker." He was holding back tears, and that fact alone made me start to panic. "K-Kelly...," he started to say and then broke down.

It took me a second to connect the name. Kyle asking me about him, Linda telling me the boy had become Kyle's quest to help... the thoughts clicked in my head a second before Brad spoke again. "Kelly shot himself" was all he could choke out before breaking down again. I covered my phone and was about to shout out for my mother when she walked in, the cordless to her ear. She was crying.

"Brad, what happened?" I asked him, knowing this was bad. He explained that during a party over winter break, someone took a video of Kelly talking to Kyle about his feelings for guys and posted it on the web for everyone to see. Kelly couldn't handle the public outing and ended up taking his own life.

As Brad explained it to me, all I could imagine was how I could have ended up like that.

In high school, I had been so terrified of someone finding out about me that I would wake up in the middle of the night in a cold sweat. My mom was talking to Mrs. Aimes, Kelly's mom. They had been friends when they lived in Foster and had kept in touch. From the way my mom was crying, she had just received the same news I had.

I calmed Brad down the best I could. He was coming apart, rambling as he told me about how Kyle had spent all winter break trying to talk Kelly down from his depression. He told me he felt as if he hadn't helped enough and that Kelly probably died hating him. He just went on and on, and I sat there and listened because he sounded like he needed a friend.

"You're coming back, right?" he asked me, his voice cracking with emotion.

I froze. His words stunned me.

"Mr. Parker, are you there?" he asked.

All the panic came rushing back again, and I was there sitting in my car watching Riley die. The old me reached up from the pit of my stomach and warned me that, if I went back now, everyone would know about me, if they didn't already. I had pushed it enough speaking up for Brad at the school board meeting; any more and I might as well stand in the middle of First Street and scream I was a fag.

I growled at my old self and said to Brad, "I'm on my way home."

I'm not sure who was more surprised to hear that I was going back to Foster, me or my parents. I began to pack my stuff when my dad came in and told me, "Your mother and I are coming too." I stared at him, confused, and he smiled. "You don't have to do this alone."

I couldn't say it out loud, but I know he saw the relief on my face.

We found a flight back to Texas the day of the funeral, which meant a lot of rushing around before we could be completely crushed with grief. My parents were changing when Brad called my phone. "Hey, we're almost there," I said assuming this was going to be a "Where are you?" call. "Give us ten minutes."

"They kicked us out," he said in a flat voice.

"What?" I asked, stammering. "Who did?"

"Kelly's dad. He blames Kyle for turning Kelly gay and wouldn't let us into the funeral home. Kyle and he got into an argument and we left."

I sat down and tried to sort out my thoughts. "Why would Kelly's dad blame Kyle?"

Brad sighed, and I could hear a car pass by in the distance. I wondered where he was but refrained from asking. "He doesn't think Kelly was gay and that Kyle put all those thoughts in his head. He really doesn't want to believe his son liked guys. I don't get it. What does it matter now that Kelly is dead?"

I didn't answer him, but I was willing to bet it mattered a lot.

"Okay, look. I need to take my parents to this thing. Why don't you two come back and we'll work it out."

He was silent for a long while. The only way I knew he hadn't hung up was because I could hear the wind through the phone. Finally he said, "I don't think so, Mr. Parker. Kyle isn't in a great place right now, and if that dick doesn't want us there, then I don't want to be there. It's better if we just stay away and let them bury Kelly in peace. We can say goodbye on our own later."

He sounded so… defeated, so resigned, it killed me. I thought I had been keeping tabs on those two and how bad it had gotten. This was just another reminder of how wrong I had been. They had been dealing with this boy all through winter break and I had no idea.

"I'm going to call you when we're done, okay?"

He sighed, and I could imagine him nodding. "Sure, Mr. Parker, whatever you want," he said and hung up.

My hands shook as I tried to keep my temper.

"We're going to be late," my dad said, coming downstairs. "Your mother is almost ready."

He didn't notice how upset I was, which was good because I didn't want to put any more on their plate than they already had. Instead I went out and warmed up the car and waited for them. Ten minutes later, my dad came out alone and got into the passenger's side. "This is about the only way I know to speed your mother up. If she knows we're both waiting out here for her, she'll hustle."

I laughed because, after all this time married, my parents still had things about each other that drove the other one crazy. You'd think they'd get used to each other's quirks and foibles, but as my dad sat there and glared at the door, it was obvious he was nowhere near that point.

"If I had killed myself when I was in high school, would you have told people I was gay?"

My father looked at me with his mouth open in shock, and I realized I might have led up to that question instead of starting there. "Come again?" he asked.

There was no way to walk that question back, so I just asked again. "Hypothetically, if I had killed myself in high school, would you have told people I was gay?"

He answered slow and measured, wary of saying something wrong, no doubt. "I didn't know you were gay in high school, so no."

"I mean, if it had come out that I was gay, and I killed myself because of it, would you have tried to deny it and tell people I was straight?"

It was a morbid question, and he had to know I was referring to Kelly, since he knew their parents pretty well. After a few moments' thought, he looked at me and admitted, "Yes."

To say the answer blew me away was an understatement.

"Would I now? No," he added. "But back then, not knowing about you? I think I would've. It would have been the absolute wrong thing to do, but I can't deny I might have done it."

Logically I knew why he would, but there was a greater part of me shocked by his answer. Of course, that part of me was a huge hypocrite since I had spent most of my life lying to and hiding the fact I was gay from every single person I knew. The fact that my father might have done the same thing wasn't as shocking as it was a comment on the world we both grew up in.

"Son," he said, putting a hand on my arm. "You know we love you no matter what, right?" I looked at him and could see in his eyes that he was desperate for me to understand what he was saying. "I am so proud of the man you have grown up to be. I wouldn't want you to change a thing about you."

"What about grandkids?" I questioned him.

He pshawed me. "You can adopt or use one of those turkey baster things the lesbians use. Just because you're gay doesn't mean you can't be cursed with children." He smiled at me, and I felt a small part of my inner fear vanish, because I realized my father did love who I had become. Inside, I had always feared he'd wished I'd turned out straight, but I could see now he was just relieved I'd made it this far.

My mom jumped into the back seat. "Okay, what are we waiting for?" she asked us impatiently.

"But don't hurry on the marriage thing," he said quietly. "Take as much time as you need for that."

Kelly's parents stood in front of the funeral home arguing quietly as we walked up. Whatever the topic was, they tabled it the moment they saw my parents.

Mrs. Aimes rushed into my mother's arms and burst out crying. My dad patted Mr. Aimes on the back and gave him condolences. Mr. Aimes turned to me and was about to say something when I asked him, "Did you really refuse to let Brad Graymark and his friend inside?"

He froze, and I could see the resentment in his eyes as he glared at me. "I did. What does that matter to you?"

"You do know you can't catch 'The Gay,' right? Kyle had nothing to do with Kelly's sexuality."

"Kelly was straight before that boy," he growled at me. "And if wasn't for that nonsense with the school board and you people raising a fuss—"

He was probably going to say more, but my father interrupted him. "When you say 'you people' you are, of course, referring to people of German descent and nothing else, right, Bill? Because I would hate it if you just referred to my son as one of 'you people.'"

Growing up, you think you've seen how angry your parents can get with you. There are screaming and yelling and spankings and days when it feels like the house is going to explode, there's so much emotion flying back and forth. You grow up thinking you know these people who raised you, that they just appeared when you were born and exist only to further your life.

And then something like this happens and you see an anger in your father's eyes so savage it takes you back a second, and you realize you might not know these people at all.

"You know what I mean, Scott. In our time, we would have never let a queer on a high school baseball team, and you know it."

My dad didn't even pause with his answer. "And in our day we had to have black kids bused in with the National Guard. We were wrong then. You are wrong now. The sad part is all this time has passed, and you're still an asshole."

"My son was not gay before all this nonsense!" he raged.

Before I had a chance to answer, his wife burst between the three of us and screamed at her husband. "You know that's not true! He was gay before all this, and we made him feel like…." She burst into tears. My mom tried to take her aside, but Mrs. Aimes shrugged the help off. "We made him feel even worse about it than he did before. You know what we did!"

We all stood there glaring at each other when the reverend came out cautiously. "We are about to begin," he said, barely above a whisper. "If you would like to come in…," he added, motioning toward the inside, silently asking the crazy people if they could stop making a scene outside and remember why we were here.

We were here because a teenager had killed himself.

We all moved indoors as the reverent silence of the funeral home took over and extinguished the argument. The Aimeses took a seat in the front pew and we sat in the middle. The service was sadder than normal because Kelly's smiling face looked back at us out of his picture on the altar. The flowery words the reverend used were lost on me. I couldn't stop looking at that picture. There were no words in the Bible that could make me okay with what had happened, no reading from scripture that could make any sense of the horrible death of someone so young.

My eyes began to blur with tears, and when I looked back up at the picture, it was of Riley. I began to openly sob.

Kelly's dad walked up and said a little speech about how proud he was when he learned he was going to be a father and how raising a son was such a challenge. His hands shook as he read off the paper he took up with him and tried not to look at the picture of his dead son. He sat down, and one of the football coaches from Foster stood up and talked about how Kelly was one of the best players he had the honor of coaching and that he was always someone he could count on in a clutch. A couple of people stood up and talked, but I had zoned out because I realized no one was talking about the real problem.

When the woman who had been talking stepped down, I stood up.

I could feel Mr. Aimes's stare drilling a hole through my head as I walked up to the podium. I hated talking in front of people, but if a kid like Brad could stand up and criticize the school board, I could at least say a few words at a funeral.

I saw all those eyes on me, and my fear screamed at me to reconsider. To sit the fuck down and live the rest of my life in silence. Be normal, be fucking normal like everyone else. Do not do this.

I silently told my fear to fuck off and began to talk.

"I didn't know Kelly personally, but I knew the kind of kid he was. He tried to run faster than the other boys, talk louder, and spit farther because he was scared. Scared that if he didn't, he'd be less of a man somehow. Those of us who are different and grow up in Foster seem to be cut from the same mold when it's time for us to learn to be men. We think that everyone else has it figured out and that if we don't know something, we should just fake it and pretend we do. We are taught that showing weakness is wrong and that if you do, you are somehow wrong. But that just isn't how life is. The dangers of small towns like this are the very things that make them wonderful to raise kids in. They give a sense of normalcy. Foster is an island of calm adrift in the middle of the insanity that the world seems to be today, and for the most part, we thank our lucky stars for that."

I could see people nodding and wiping their eyes, and I forced myself to keep talking.

"Our town has been spared things like gangs and real crime. We don't have shootings or a drug problem. We are safe here and secure that our kids are safe. We love this town because of that, but it comes at a price, a price that unfortunately Kelly had to pay."

People gasped, but I pressed on.

"What happened was a tragedy, but it was one that could have been avoided if we just realized what we were doing to these kids." I looked at Mr. Aimes. "Kelly may have pulled the trigger, but it was the rest of us who put the gun in his hands."

Aimes jumped out of his seat, screaming, as people began to talk hurriedly to each other.

"There is nothing wrong with being gay," I said, talking over the chaos. "I'm gay, and I should have said that before. I am as much to blame as anyone else is. We are all to blame. We need to have a real conversation in this town about what being a man is and how it's okay to be different."

"My son was not gay!" Mr. Aimes stood up and yelled.

"And if he was," I said to him from behind the podium, "there would have been nothing wrong with that." I looked to the crowd, who was captivated by the real-life drama in front of them. "I am Tyler Parker, and I am gay. I have always been gay and just too terrified to admit it. The entire time you have known me, I liked guys. I am the exact same person who was born and raised in this town and who you all cheered for when I went off to college." I pointed to myself. "I am the same guy you rooted for in the bleachers, and I am the same guy you buy your kid's uniforms from. I am a gay man, and not one of you had a problem with me the entire time I lived here." I took a deep breath and asked them, "So why would you now?"

I looked at Mr. Aimes. "Why should they have a problem with Kelly? With Brad or Kyle or with *any* kid in this town? It doesn't matter what they are or who they are attracted to. They are our kids, and shouldn't that be enough for us to let them be who they want to be?"

"How dare you embarrass my son like this?" Mr. Aimes raged at me.

"He's dead," I said to him, shaking my head. "He isn't embarrassed. That is you. Are you incapable of seeing anything past your own ego? This isn't them!" I finally shouted. "They get it from us. *We* are the ones with the problem, and we pass it along to them. If there is going to be a solution, it needs to come from us. How many more kids need to kill themselves before we realize that something needs to change around here?" No one answered, but that's okay. I didn't expect them to. I opened my mouth to say more, but I looked up and saw him in the doorway and my brain just froze.

Matt stood there and smiled at me.

"I just wanted to say that. I'm gay and none of you had a problem with me before." I looked at Mr. Aimes. "And they wouldn't have had a problem with Kelly either."

I didn't wait for their reaction; instead, I walked down the aisle toward Matt, no longer even caring where I was or who was watching. I reached out to him and pulled him into a kiss that made my entire world shake from his presence. I knew everyone in the room was watching us kiss, but all I cared about was this man in my arms and how he made me feel.

The kiss lasted for what felt like hours before I was able to remove my mouth from his. My forehead was pressed against his as I combated the twin urges to cry and laugh at the same time. "I'm sorry," I said, not able to look him in the eye yet.

"And I'm Matt," he whispered back. "I don't think we've met." That made me look up, and I saw the tears sliding down his cheeks. "But I would love the chance to know you."

I nodded as my brain flooded my mouth with far too many responses for anything to be considered English.

Someone called out "Kiss him again!" and I heard laughter rumble through the room. I looked back and saw everyone was looking at us. Most of them were crying, except this time they were tears of joy.

Before we walked out, I looked at the picture of Kelly again. For the first time in a long time, I didn't see Riley's ghost looking back at me.

MATT

WE SAT in my car as the people shuffled out of the funeral home.

"I'm not complaining, but how are you here?" he asked me.

I had been dreading that question ever since I decided to move back to Foster. There was no way I could convey to him that I did not move back here with some creepy plan to stalk him all over again.

"I live here now," I finally admitted. "Not because of you, if that's what you're scared of." He tried to interrupt me, but I kept talking. "I wasn't happy there. I haven't been happy anywhere, and I needed to be honest about that for once. I kept thinking that if I moved somewhere or did different things, I was going to end up happy somehow, but it wasn't true. I am unhappy, and I bring that with me wherever I go. So I moved back in with my parents and am going to try to figure out who the hell I am."

He smiled at me, and I resisted the urge to ask him what he was thinking.

"I've felt that way since high school," he admitted to me.

That made me laugh. "Yeah, I figured."

We both asked at once, "So now what?"

We chuckled at that for a few seconds before I said, "Okay, we tried love at first sight and we tried chasing each other halfway across the country. How about we try it from the beginning?" He arched an eyebrow questioningly as I stuck out my hand. "My name is Matt, and I used to watch you read as you leaned against your red door."

He took my hand slowly. "I'm Tyler, and I used to watch you watching me." That made me redden a little, and he added, "There's a gay bar on the outskirts of town. It's not fancy, but it's a place to go. Would you like to go have a drink with me?"

I stared at him for a moment, wondering if he was playing with me or not. After a long pause, I nodded. "That sounds like a date."

Warmth made it all the way down to my toes as he answered, "It *is* a date."

It wasn't an explosion or a burst of fireworks; it was something slower and far more powerful. As we sat there waiting for the parking lot to empty, I could feel the continental plates that made up my life begin to shift under me. And it hit me....

This was the moment my life truly began. This was the day I stopped running from being happy and just let it happen.

And for the first time in my life, that wasn't a bad thing.

NOT THE end....

POSTSCRIPT

LOVE IS hard.

I don't say that like I have cured cancer or figured how many licks it takes to get into a Tootsie Roll Pop or anything, but it is worth stating. Love is hard; real love is even harder. No matter how many times boy A meets girl B in a movie and falls in love while the catchy pop tune of the moment plays behind them, it doesn't make it real. Hollywood has made love incredibly simple and impossibly difficult in the same action by trying to convince us that love is what they show us.

Simple because we think you meet someone, fall in love, and all is well. Impossible because you rarely meet someone, fall in love, and then all is well. We are sold these fairy tales by the pound and eat them up with a spoon day after day, TV show after TV show, movie after movie. There are whole industries making people believe that love is simple, love is obvious, and love comes for everyone.

Not everyone gets to fall in love.

I know, not a popular statement, but as with my first proclamation, it needs to be said out loud. Love is so much more than just the right moment and the right song and the right place. Saying it is like that is like saying that cooking is just putting stuff in a pot and hoping it comes out as a meal. Sure it *can* happen, but how many bad meals can you make before you realize there might be more to cooking than that?

Now this may sound like I am anti-love, but that isn't true. I am a big fan of love. I am all pro-love. Me and love are… well, I was going to say in love, but we are at best close, personal friends. There is a third proclamation coming up, so be ready, because like the other two, it isn't rocket science.

Gay love is even harder.

I know, duh, right?

Let's go back to the cooking analogy, because I am too lazy to come up with a new one. So putting random ingredients in a pot and cooking it does not make a meal. Now consider you are not just trying to make a meal doing that, you are trying to make a meal that is low sodium, gluten free, and has under a hundred calories a serving. Suddenly the chances of all that crap you threw in the pot becoming something edible seems impossible, doesn't it? All this is just talking to the numbers of falling in love. There are so many people out there, only so many gay people, only so many gay people who you will find attractive, only so many you would be compatible with, and then only so many of those who you would have the opportunity to meet.

This isn't even taking into account the slut factor.

Now before I go on, this is *not* something all gay men go through. It is not a law, it is not even a statement, it is simply something I have observed and had other gay men agree with me on. So if you do not agree with me, that is fine; skip down a few paragraphs. There is a cute thing with Michael Jackson at the end.

Gay men are a lot like people who have been starved for most of their lives, forced to watch other people eat whenever they want.

Man, food again. I think I might be hungry.

Growing up, we see boy and girl, boy and girl, boy and girl over and over again until we are ready to scream. Most of us are not ready to announce our gayness to the world, and even if we do, the odds of someone in high school being gay is so rare it isn't even worth talking about sometimes. So we spend most of high school sitting outside the restaurant of love, watching other couples eat what we so desperately crave. Sometimes even in college we can't sack up, so we go even longer starving ourselves. Sometimes we will pretend, just to be with anyone. Sometimes we will sneak around and take random thrills in the night, just to keep from going crazy. Either way, it is not a good thing.

Once we are out of school, away from home, away from the people who think we're someone we aren't, we tend to go a little nuts. How nuts? Try putting a group of people who have not eaten in years in an all-you-can-eat buffet and tell me how many of them are deciding to eat healthy. We binge, we try everything, we try to shove all those lost years into the smallest possible window of time.

In other words, we kind of turn into sluts.

Not everyone, and not everywhere, to be sure. But in general, most gay guys have been or at least know a slut or two. So there we are, in our sex buffet, going nuts and growing older. That elusive quality all young men have begins to fade, and we come out of our calorie-induced coma and wonder *What am I going to do now?* We've had sex, a lot of sex, and in some cases more than a lot; we've done the club thing; we've done the casual fun thing. What about the love thing?

And then, most of the time, we get stupid.

Remember our pot we were just throwing shit into earlier? Yeah, well, you have to remember that most straight people have been at least pretending to cook most of their lives. They grew up knowing what their whole role was going to be. Some girls wanted to be a princess, some wanted to be an astronaut, some wanted to raise a family, some wanted to take over the world, and guys did the same thing. Some of us wanted to pretend we were in *Swingers* and everything was Vegas, baby! And some of us watched *The Notebook* and realized there was nothing wrong with being a romantic. But through popular media, the culture, the people around you, you began to shape what you would someday dream of.

For some of us, we just made it up as we went along.

Some tried to date guys like we saw other guys date girls. Some of us rejected the heterosexual model and took a more open lifestyle approach. And some guys just figured it out and settled down without a peep. It's confusing to be a middle-aged gay man and not know what's next. Am I supposed to want to marry someone? Am I supposed to adopt a kid? Do I have to watch *Glee* every week even if I hate musicals? We fumble around in the dark for so long, looking for a light, that we just forget the point.

That we are not happy and want to be happy.

This book is about the messiness of gay relationships. There is no promise that Matt and Tyler will work out, which is why there is not a "The End." Just finding someone you like isn't the end; it's just the beginning of an even stranger and more challenging phase of a gay man's life.

And this is why we need role models.

This very reason is why we, as a culture, must fight for gay people to be fairly represented in media. Why we should celebrate shows like *Glee*, *The New Normal*, *Modern Family*, and many, many others that show there is a way to be gay, happy, and in a relationship. We need to start showing gay teenagers out there right now that this isn't a bad thing, this isn't a weird thing… this is a life thing.

So if you are gay and not sure where you are in your life, it's okay. Trust me, it's okay. Take a deep breath and remember, it's about being happy. And that starts with being happy with you. This is not as hard as it looks. Sure, it may look like those people are just throwing things into a pot and making food, but trust me.

They've had a cookbook much longer than we have. We'll get there.

—John Goode 2021

JOHN GOODE is fifty years old and was found in his floating crib by a strange man… wait, no that's Baby Yoda. I am a cat that gets constantly screamed at by a blond woman while I'm trying to eat… wait, no, not me. I am inevitable, nope. I am Iron Man? More no. I'm not bad, I'm just drawn that way? I can't pull that dress off. Okay, I am and shall always be your friend. Sigh, I think I stole that from somewhere. Let me try again. WHEN I WAS A YOUNG WARTHOG! Too much? I agree. Okay, how about a little Fosse, Fosse, Fossee, a little Martha Graham, Martha Graham, Twyla, Twyla, Twyla and then some Michael Kidd, Michael… I lost you, huh? Well whoever he is, I can assure you he isn't a black cat that wears glasses. Okay, how about this?

He is this guy who lives in this place and writes stuff he hopes you read.

Twitter: @fosterhigh
Facebook: www.facebook.com/TalesFromFosterHigh

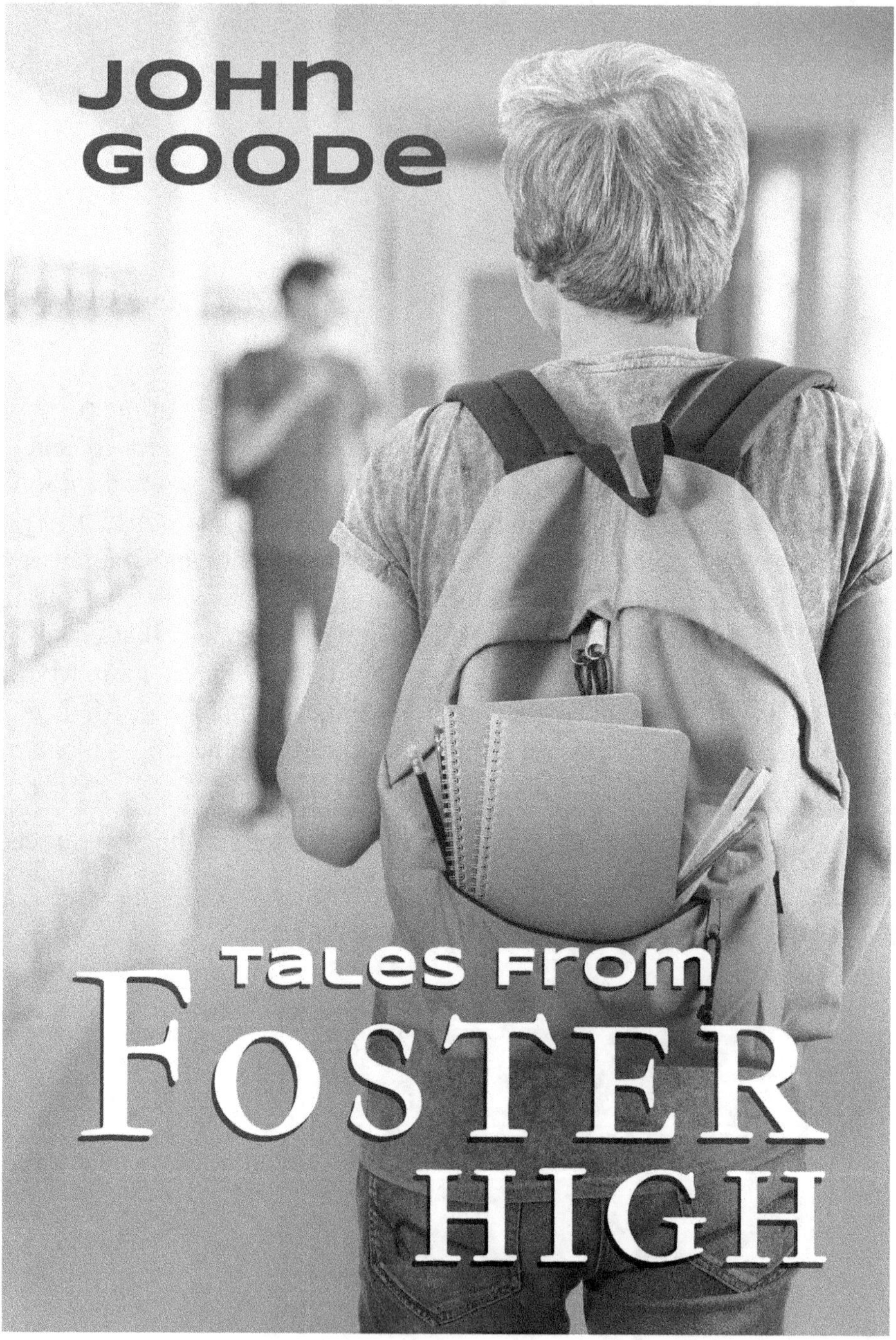
JOHN
GOODE
TALES FROM
FOSTER
HIGH

Tales from Foster High: Book One

Kyle Stilleno is the invisible student even in his nothing high school in the middle of Nowhere, Texas. Brad Graymark is the baseball star of Foster High. When they bond over their mutual damage during a night of history tutoring, Kyle thinks maybe his life has changed for good. But when you're gay and falling for the most popular boy in school, the promise of love is a fairy tale, not a reality. Isn't it?

A coming-of-age story, *Tales from Foster High* shows an unflinching vision of the ups and downs of teenage love and what it is like to grow up gay.

www.dreamspinnerpress.com

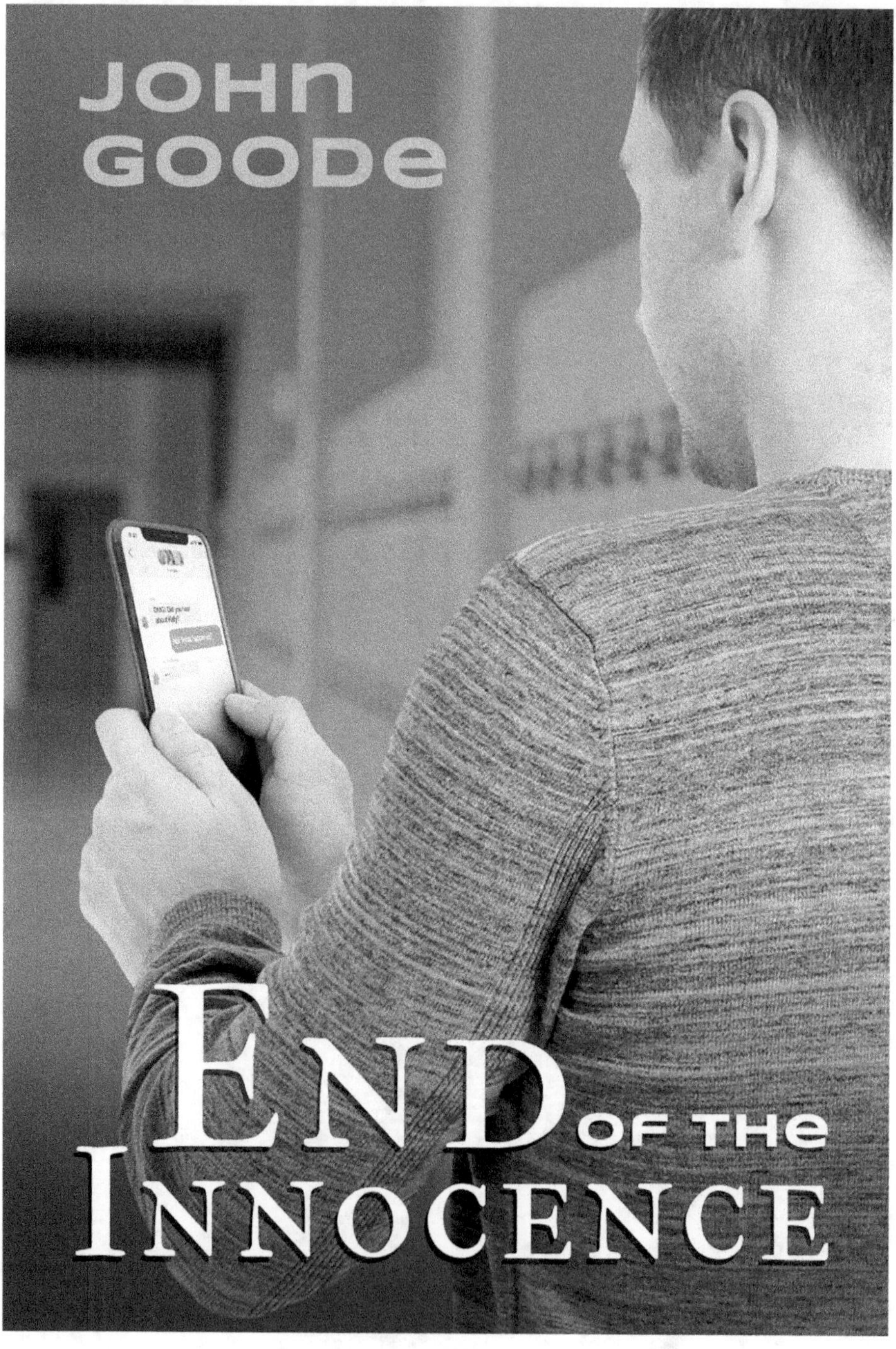
JOHN
GOODE
END OF THE
INNOCENCE

Tales from Foster High: Book Two

Kyle Stilleno is no longer the invisible boy, and he doesn't know how he feels about it. On one hand, he now has a great boyfriend, Brad Graymark, a handful of new friends, and even a new job. On the other hand, no one screamed obscenities at him in public when he was invisible.

No one expected him to become a poster boy for gay rights either— at least not until he stepped out of the closet and into the limelight. But with only a few months of high school left, Kyle doubts he can make a difference.

With Christmas break drawing closer and their trials far from over, Kyle and Brad have each other to lean on. Others are not so lucky. One of their classmates needs their help—but Kyle and Brad's relationship may be too new to survive the strain.

www.dreamspinnerpress.com

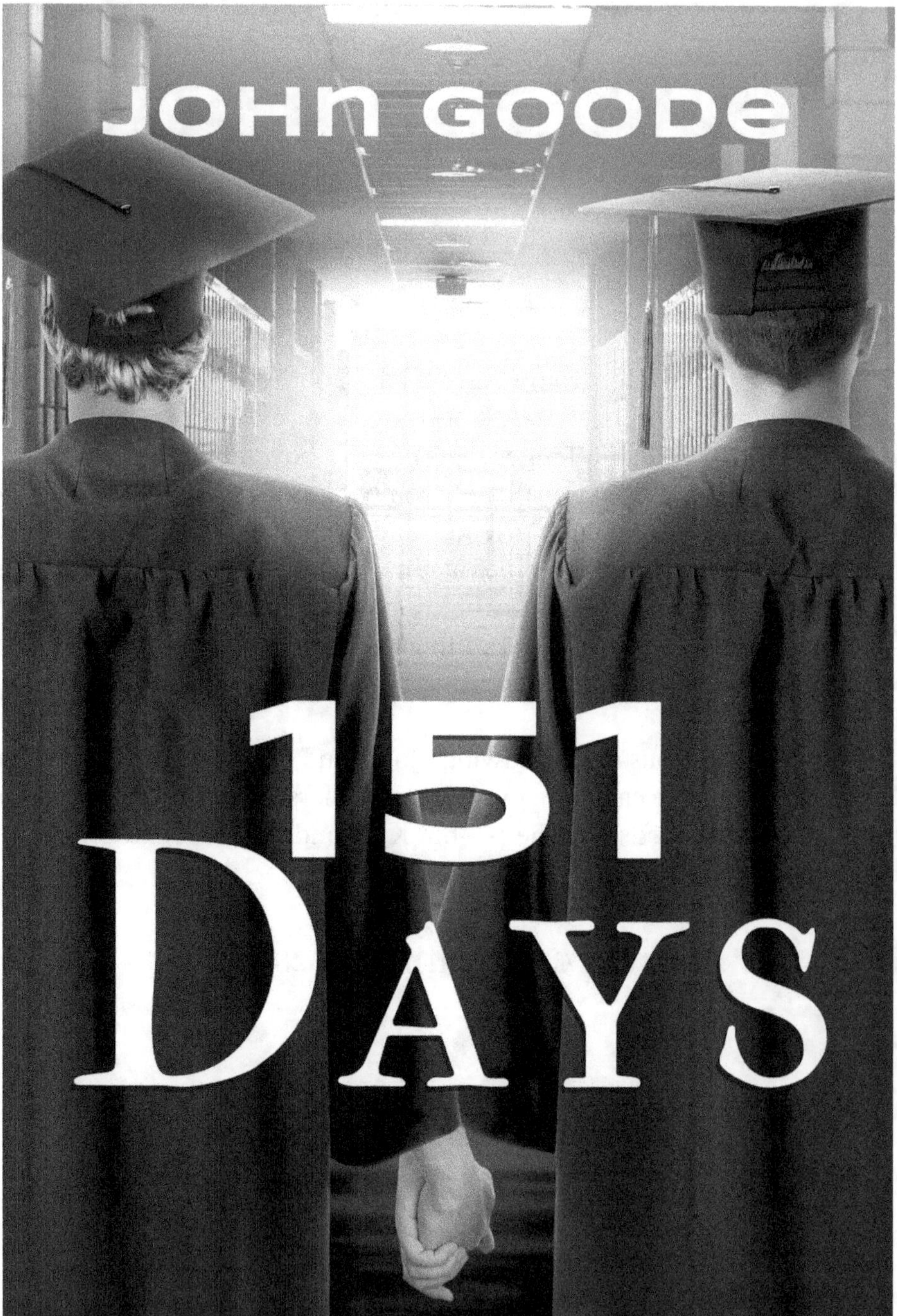
JOHN GOODE
151
DAYS

Tales from Foster High: Book Three

With just 151 days left until the school year ends, Kyle Stilleno is running out of time to fulfill the promise he made and change Foster, Texas, for the better. But he and his boyfriend, Brad Graymark, have more than just intolerance to deal with. Life, college, love, and sex have a way of distracting them, and they're realizing Foster is a bigger place than they thought. When someone from their past returns at the worst possible moment, graduation becomes the least of their worries.

www.dreamspinnerpress.com